A Whisker Away

A Klepto Cat Mystery

Patricia Fry

A Whisker Away

A Klepto Cat Mystery

by Patricia Fry

ISBN 978-1-7369430-2-1

This novel is a work of fiction. The characters, names, incidents, dialogue are the products of the author's imagination or are used fictitiously. Any resemblance to actual persons, companies or events is purely coincidental.

Cover Art: Bernadette E. Kazmarski

Cover layout: Dennis Mullican
Page layout: Dennis Mullican

Printed in U.S.A. by: KDP

A Whisker Away

A Klepto Cat Mystery

Book 52

It was a pretty winter morning in San Francisco, and Savannah Ivey was eager to get home after an interesting and eventful few days with investigative reporter, Parker Campbell. The two women and their cats, Rags and Olivia, had teamed up to help a group of women save a decades-old cat colony. Savannah and Parker knew there was a secret buried in the wooded area where the feral cats lived, but they were stunned to learn the horrible truth. Savannah was still reeling from the shock of their grim discovery.

She massaged one of Rags's paws as he lay on the car seat next to her. "That was quite an intense few days, wasn't it, boy? You and Olivia were awesome." She smiled briefly at the cat as she drove. "You two sure hit it off, but then you're pretty mellow when it comes to other cats." She chuckled. "It's kind of cat week for you. We'll stop at Rochelle's and Peter's house before heading home, and you'll get to see Minnie and Blossom. You remember them—the kittens we found that Christmas season when we took Simon and Rochelle on a horseback ride. You met the kittens when they were tiny, but you haven't seen them very often since they've grown up." Giggling, she added, "Blossom actually looks a little like you, only she's fluffier and a lighter shade of grey. Well, here we are, Rags. Are you ready for a visit? Rochelle and I are going to have lunch, then you and I will head for home sweet home."

When Rags raised his head and mewed Savannah said, "Yeah, I'm eager to get home, too. I sure do miss everyone, but we should take advantage of being down here in the big city and visit with our good friends, right?"

***

"Savannah!" Rochelle squealed, approaching her as she stepped out of the car. Rochelle tilted her head. "Whose car is this?"

"Mom's," Savannah said. "I leave my car with the kids' car seats for her when I go off somewhere by myself."

Rochelle peered into the car. "I see you have Rags's car seat." She ruffled the cat's fur as he sat looking at her from the driver's seat. Why aren't you riding in there, Rags?"

"We didn't have far to go," Savannah explained. "We've been staying in a condo only about fifteen or twenty miles from here." She ran her hand over Rags's fur. "Sometimes it's just easier to let him lounge on the seat. He'll be restrained for our long drive home this afternoon, though."

"Well, come in. Are you hungry?"

"Almost," Savannah said, picking up the cat. She grinned. "Did you cook?"

Rochelle shook her head. "No. I have a better idea—something fun for us. At least I'm looking forward to it."

"Oh?" Savannah questioned.

"Yeah. It's such a nice day I thought the cats would like to go to the park."

"The cats?" Savannah repeated.

"Yes," Rochelle said. "Are you up for a picnic with the cats?"

"Well, that sounds nice," Savannah said, "but I didn't know you took your cats out like that."

"We do now," Rochelle said. "Simon has done an excellent job of leash-training them, and…"

Savannah interrupted. "They're leash-trained? Do you mean they walk along nicely with you like a dog?"

"Not exactly," Rochelle said, chuckling, "but they will wear a harness and a leash, and they will sometimes walk with us. That's as far as Simon has gotten with them."

"And that's probably as far as you're going to get," Savannah said, laughing. "They *are* cats, after all. But yes, a picnic with the cats sounds nice."

"Come in," Rochelle invited. "Need to wash up?"

Savannah grinned at her. "I just drove a few miles. I'm fine."

"Okay, then. Let me grab my jacket and the picnic basket."

"So you *did* make lunch," Savannah said, following Rochelle into the house.

"No. I ordered sandwiches at my favorite deli—actually one turkey sandwich cut in half, two orders of salad, and two of their giant oatmeal-raisin cookies." She motioned toward the basket. "I packed plates, silverware, napkins, tablecloth…"

"Candelabra?" Savannah joked. She laughed at the vision, then added, "A deli sandwich and salad sound great. Will there be coffee?"

"If that's what you want, of course. How about we take my car," Rochelle offered, "since you have that long drive home this afternoon?"

"And since you know where you're going," Savannah added. When she saw a fluffy grey-and-white cat saunter into the room, she greeted, "Hi, Blossom. How are you, sweetie? She has really blossomed, Rochelle." She giggled. "Sorry, I couldn't help the pun." She asked, while petting Blossom, "Was that actually a pun or just a play on words? Or is there a difference?" She glanced up at Rochelle and frowned. "Is something wrong? Rochelle!" she said more loudly. When Rochelle jumped and turned to look at her, Savannah asked,

"Where were you, girl? What do you have on your mind? Hey, did I barge in at a bad time?"

"No!" Rochelle assured her. "No, I'm okay. It's just one of those days for me. I have something sort of bothering me, but there's really no basis for it." She laughed and pointed above her head. "Do you see the dark cloud following me around?"

"Rochelle, what's going on? Tell me."

"Oh, nothing really. It's just a sort of lingering sense—you know, leftover from a dream. I don't want to talk about it or think about it. I'm okay. Let's go on with our day, shall we? I really am looking forward to our time together. Here," she said, tossing Savannah a cat harness, "want to put this on Blossom? You're definitely more experienced than I am. Simon's the expert around here."

"Sure," Savannah said, kneeling. She picked up the cat and cuddled with her for a moment, then lowered her to the sofa. She easily slipped the harness around her and fastened it.

Rochelle looked down at Blossom. "Well, that went well. I usually have to chase her down and wrestle her to the ground."

"Really?" Savannah asked, hooking the leash to Blossom's harness. "I guess I caught her off guard."

"I guess you did," Rochelle said. She ruffled the fur on the cat's head and crooned. "Are you ready to go on an adventure, sweet girl?" She stood up; grabbed the basket, a jacket, and her shoulder purse; then asked, "Can you manage both cats?"

"Sure. Come on, Blossom," Savannah urged, taking her leash. "You remember Rags, don't you? He was the first cat you met after we rescued you and your sister. Rags is going on an adventure with us today. Are you up for it?" She chuckled. "Or would you rather laze around on satin tending to your long, silky fur?" She looked at Rochelle. "She *is* a beauty. Hey, where's Minnie? Did her fur ever grow out fluffy like Blossom's?"

"No," Rochelle said. She pointed. "Here she comes. See, she's the short-hair version of Blossom."

"I see that. Minnie, you're sleek and beautiful. What a lovely and lucky pair of cats," Savannah said. "I mean, when we found them they were probably less than an hour away from being some coyote's or hawk's lunch." She shuddered at the thought.

"Don't even think that," Rochelle insisted. "Poor babies being dumped in the hills all alone—I can't even imagine someone doing that."

"But look at them now," Savannah said enthusiastically. "They don't have a care in the world."

"I doubt they had a care then, either," Rochelle said. "The poor tiny beings didn't have an inkling of where they were or what danger they were in."

Savannah nodded. "I think you're right. Well, they certainly are lucky, lucky kitty-cats."

"And so are we," Rochelle said, "lucky, that is. We really do love them."

"Peter too?" Savannah asked, grinning. "Have they turned him around—I mean, from someone who wasn't all that fond of cats?"

"That's putting it mildly," Rochelle said, "but oh yes, they have won him over heart and soul."

"Heart and soul?" Savannah questioned.

Rochelle grinned. "Well, he lets them sleep on our bed and sit on the furniture."

"That's a leap. Good for him," Savannah said.

"And good for the rest of us. It was pretty uncomfortable there for a while until Peter stopped complaining about cats in the house, fur all over his slacks, litter scattered around…" Rochelle said.

"How did you get him to stop complaining?" Savannah asked. "I still have a complaining husband—sometimes, anyway."

Rochelle squinted at her thoughtfully. "Now that you mention it, I guess he still complains, but his complaints have a significantly different tone and connotation. Yeah, he's not all that wild about the inconveniences and negatives of having cats in the house, but he isn't as vocal. I think that's because he enjoys them so much. He's learned that there's a lot of good stuff going on to offset the inconveniences."

"Nice to hear it," Savannah said.

Once the women and the cats were in the car and on their way, Rochelle said, "I hope you don't mind, I have a stop to make. I told Simon I'd drop off the application and fee for his 4-H membership. The first meeting is this weekend, and he wants to make sure he's accepted."

"Why wouldn't he be?" Savannah asked.

"No reason, really. It's just about his comfort level," Rochelle explained. "He's a kid who likes to map things out before taking the next step. He wants to cover his bases." She glanced at Savannah. "He works hard at avoiding uncomfortable situations. I guess he had enough of those in his former life before we adopted him. It's not a bad practice, only I worry sometimes that he won't be willing to take risks—you know, be spontaneous, even vulnerable. I think it's important to know how to do that. We all feel vulnerable at times, and we must learn how to deal with it. Do you know what I mean?"

"I think so. Planning ahead is a good practice, but I agree, we need to help our children also learn to be flexible. Not everything goes our way all the time. We will be met with disappointments, surprises, and change. Those things happen, and we have to be somewhat prepared to deal with them."

Rochelle nodded and spoke more quietly, "Yeah, surprises can be frightening, even when you know one may be coming."

"What?" Savannah asked, frowning.

"Oh nothing," Rochelle said, shaking her head. She took a deep breath. "There's a quote I hear a lot these days, you probably do too. I think it's becoming a sort of coping mechanism for people facing those unpleasant surprises." She quoted, 'It is what it is.'"

Savannah laughed. "Yeah, that's certainly a popular modern-day mantra, isn't it?" She asked, "So will Simon raise a steer or a pig or something?"

"Maybe in the future, but this 4-H group has an avian program. He wants to learn more about birds—our birds and wild birds. He hopes to enter Clayton and Matilda in the county fair this year."

"Really?" Savannah said. "How *are* the parrots?"

"Doing great," Rochelle said. "Simon sure enjoys them. He's continually teaching Clayton new words." She laughed. "I sometimes hear him out at the aviary repeating a word or a phrase over and over and over, ad nauseam," she exaggerated.

"That's what it takes," Savannah said. She added, "So the lost parrots Rags and I found in that park will become show birds? That's an interesting concept. I don't think I've ever seen a bird exhibit at a county fair, other than chickens and ducks and geese, maybe. Good for Simon. It's great seeing him get so involved in animals."

"And sports," Rochelle said. "He played baseball last season, and he's looking forward to playing again this year. He also wants to sign up for basketball." She glanced at Savannah as she drove. "I think Adam had something to do with that."

"Good. I know that Adam's mom and stepdad have him in at least a couple of sports. I think those recreational sports programs are good for boys, and for girls. Kids have the opportunity to learn all kinds of skills and lessons—how to be a team player, a gracious winner and loser, and so much more. I'm also glad to hear that the boys still talk. I think there's a lot they can learn from each other."

"I agree. They talk even more since they both have cell phones." Rochelle turned onto a small country road and frowned into the rearview mirror.

"What's wrong?" Savannah asked, looking behind them.

"I hope nothing. It's just that I'm starting to get the distinct feeling that guy's following us."

"Really? Maybe you have a low tire, a loose hubcap, or a seat belt hanging out," Savannah suggested.

Rochelle grinned impishly. "Do people really go that far out of their way to help someone else? Anyway, I'm pretty sure he's been behind us practically since we left home. If there was something wrong, wouldn't he have honked or blinked his lights at us by now?"

"Well, we'll find out if he's following us when we stop at the 4-H leader's house, right?" Savannah giggled. "Maybe he lives there."

Rochelle kept an eye on her mirror and nodded, then she relaxed a little. "I guess I'm being a little paranoid. There he goes on his merry way up the road."

"You, paranoid?" Savannah asked, surprised. "Why would you be paranoid?"

"Oh, um…" Rochelle stammered. "No real reason, I guess." She glanced around. "It's just that, who would have thought two people would leave our tract in separate cars at the same time, and both be visiting someone out here on the same backcountry road?" She squinted into the distance. "Looks like he's going to the house at the end of the road." She opened her car door and stepped out, calling, "Be right back."

***

The women had been sitting at a partially shaded picnic table in the park eating lunch and chatting for about forty-five minutes when Rochelle lowered her head and her voice. "Oh no, there he is again."

"Who?" Savannah asked, following Rochelle's gaze to the parking lot.

"I don't know, but…" She took a breath. "Kiddo, I have a creepy feeling."

"What's going on, Rochelle?" Savannah asked. "What has you so spooked? Do you know who that guy is?"

Rochelle shook her head. "I don't think so, but the car—Savannah, I've seen that car every night in my sleep for pretty close to a week. When I saw it behind us earlier—I mean, that just about put me under, and now here it is again."

"Well, Rochelle," Savannah said, "black sedans are not uncommon. Are you sure you're seeing the same car, or are you just noticing that type of car—you know, you have it in your head, so you notice it?"

"I don't think so," Rochelle said. "I'm pretty sure it's the same car and that it's significant somehow."

"Significant in what way," Savannah asked, "in the type of car or the color?"

Rochelle shrugged and tried to avoid looking in the direction of the car as it moved slowly through the parking lot.

"He could be looking for someone," Savannah said. She pointed. "That woman over there seems to be alone with her dog. Maybe her husband or boyfriend is checking up on her."

"Maybe, but why would I have dreams about that car, and why would I suddenly begin to see it when I'm wide awake?" Rochelle asked.

"I don't know." Savannah chuckled. "*You're* the psychic." When she could see that her friend was not in the mood for frivolity, she asked more seriously, “What were your thoughts when you dreamed about that car, Rochelle?”

“They were more like nightmares,” Rochelle said, “not dreams. What were my thoughts?” she repeated. “I don’t recall thoughts, just emotions—fear, terror. Oh yes, nothing good. That’s why it freaked me out to see him behind us in such a rural area earlier.” Rochelle rested her head in her hands. “Then there are the phone calls. Someone keeps calling and hanging up as soon as I answer.”

“Oh, Rochelle,” Savannah said, “everyone gets those calls. I’m sure they’re just robocalls.” She frowned. “Rochelle, I don’t believe I’ve ever seen you so shaken. What’s really going on?”

Rochelle shook her head. “I don’t know. I just don’t know, but I don’t feel safe. I sense that I’m on the verge of something awful—something I’m powerless to stop.”

“Really?” Savannah questioned, beginning to feel a bit uneasy herself.

“Yeah. You know that I have premonitions.”

“Of course, and I love you anyway,” Savannah joked.

Rochelle glanced at her, then gazed toward the parking lot again. “Well, I can often warn someone of impending danger and help them to stop something bad from happening, or maybe prepare them for something that’s about to happen, but not generally when it comes to myself.” In a pinched voice, she said, "I sense that I'm in danger, and that I do not have the ability to stop whatever is destined to happen. I feel such a sense of doom."

Not sure how to respond, Savannah scanned the parking lot. "Well, that black car seems to have left. He's gone." She rested a hand on Rochelle's arm and soothed, "I'm so sorry you're going through this. It must be awful for you, but girl, you've gotta get a grip."

"I agree," Rochelle said. "I'm working on it, but so far I'm really kind of scared."

Just then Savannah caught a glimpse of Rags. *Uh-oh,* she thought. *What has him on alert?* She watched him for a minute. *Dang, I hope he doesn't sense what Rochelle senses, and I hope she doesn't notice him acting all worked up like that.* She tugged on the cat's leash to bring him closer and began petting him under the table, then asked, "Rochelle, have you told Peter about this?"

She shook her head. "I don't want to worry him unnecessarily."

Savannah sat up straighter and said with emphasis, "There, you said it, Rochelle."

"Said what?" she asked.

"You don't want to worry Peter *unnecessarily*—without reason. But in the meantime, you're really doing a number on yourself, aren't you?"

"Yes, I am," Rochelle admitted. She smiled hesitantly. "I'm sorry, Savannah. I didn't mean to…"

"No apologies necessary, girlfriend." Savannah looked under the table at Rags, who had settled down a little. She ran her hand over his head and down his back, then said to Rochelle, "I'm here for you. You know that. I just hope you can shake this sense of dread before it interferes with your beautiful life as a mom, and a wife, and an amazing jewelry artist."

"It won't interfere with my life," Rochelle said. "I won't let it."

Savannah winced. "Hon, I think it already has. Look at you. You're a nervous wreck. Rochelle, I've never seen you like this. You're usually Ms. Cucumber."

"Cucumber?" Rochelle challenged.

"As in 'cool as,'" Savannah explained.

Both women laughed, and Rochelle said, "I know you're right. I need to get a grip, and I'm sure going to try." She asked more quietly, "So you think he's gone?"

Savannah gazed toward the parking lot. "Seems to be."

Rochelle visibly relaxed. She reached her hand into a small bag. "Hey, want a cookie?"

"Sheesh," Savannah said when Rochelle pulled one out. "They're big. How about splitting one with me?"

"Sure," Rochelle agreed. She jumped a little, then laughed. "Blossom, what are you doing?"

Savannah looked down at the cat. "What did she do?"

"She clawed me," Rochelle said. She peered under the table. "Hey, both Blossom and Rags are after my feet. Stop it, you two!"

Savannah chuckled. "Maybe you stepped in something yummy and they want a lick of it."

"Do you think so?" Rochelle asked, lifting one foot. "I don't see anything. Hey, wait. It's that piece of paper they're after. I guess I was stepping on it. What is that?" She picked it up and studied it. "Now that's odd."

"What?" Savannah asked, taking her last sip of coffee.

"It appears to be a treasure map."

Savannah raised her eyebrows. "No kidding. Let me see." After looking at it for a few moments, she handed it back to Rochelle. "It's probably for a child's birthday party or something. Hey, what a cool idea—a treasure hunt at a park. Lily and Teddy would have fun with that, although they'd need help reading and following the clues. Where does it lead to?" she asked.

"Well…" Rochelle started. She turned the map around and looked across the park, pointing.

"Do you think that tree is the one depicted on this map? It looks like that's where the first clue is…or was." Excitedly, she asked, "Want to go look?"

"Sure. Come on, Rags. You'd probably be a good treasure hunter." She laughed and said to Rochelle, "However, he'd probably run around snatching up all the clues and prizes before the kids could even play the game."

Rochelle gazed at Rags as the women and the cats walked toward the tree together. "Do you think so? Rags are you a spoilsport?" After scouring the area around the tree, she said, "Well, I don't see anything here. Shouldn't there be another clue?" She then said, "Wait. Is that an arrow? Does that look like an arrow to you?"

"Where?" Savannah asked.

"Rags just sat on it. Move, Rags," Rochelle insisted, nudging him.

"Yes," Savannah said. "I think you're right. It looks like those sticks were arranged in the shape of an arrow before Rags messed with them."

"What direction do you think it's supposed to point?" Rochelle asked.

After studying the stick formation from several angles, Savannah said, "That way. Over toward those bushes."

Rochelle nodded. "I think you're right. Come on," she said, tugging on Blossom's leash. When the cat wouldn't follow, she picked her up. "Let's go see what's in that azalea bush over there." She shimmied. "I can't wait for them to start blooming. This park is so beautiful when the azaleas and rhododendrons are blooming."

"I can imagine," Savannah said. She asked, "Didn't Peter do a painting of a grassy area with flowering shrubs all around? Was that here?"

"Yes," Rochelle said. "That's one of my favorites of his paintings, which makes this park one of my favorite parks." She squinted into the bushes. "Do you see anything?"

Savannah shook her head. When Rags dove into the undergrowth of a shrub she said, "Well, just barge on in, Rags. What in the heck are you after?"

"A lizard!" Rochelle squealed, stumbling backward.

The women laughed when Blossom leaped from Rochelle's arms, and both cats chased the lizard back into the bush.

"No!" Rochelle shouted, reaching for her cat. "Oops," she yelped when she picked up Blossom. "Your fur got all tangled in the bushes." She grimaced. "Blossom, you are not designed to chase lizards into dense brush." She chuckled and said to Savannah, "I think she left a piece of her behind."

"Oh no, Miss Fluffy Pants," Savannah said, plucking the puff of fur from the bough. "Look what you lost." She dropped it back into the shrub and smiled. "Some bird will appreciate having that for her nest in the spring." She picked up Rags and quipped, "Well, Rochelle, do you think that's the treasure—a lizard?"

"The cats thought so," Rochelle said, laughing.

"What else is on the map?" Savannah asked.

"Well, it shows a rock." She looked around and repeated, "Rock. What rock?"

"Oh, there," Savannah pointed. "Is that it—the one next to our picnic table? The cats were showing an interest in that rock a while ago. If there was a treasure near there, Rags and Blossom probably found it and ate it."

"X marks the spot," Rochelle said when they approached the rock. "See the X drawn on the back of it here? She picked up a smaller rock. I'll bet they used this to make that mark."

"So is the treasure under the rock?" Savannah asked.

"Actually, I doubt there's any treasure at the end of this rainbow," Rochelle said. "Don't you think that map is a leftover from a party that happened last weekend or something? The game's probably long over."

Savannah giggled. "So why are we out here like fools chasing after a treasure?"

"I'm sure there's a reason," Rochelle said. "We're getting our exercise. And I'm getting my mind off that…" she shuddered. Suddenly she shrieked, "Blossom, now what?"

Savannah turned to see Blossom run past her with Rochelle close behind. Rochelle made a grab for the cat's leash, but Blossom quickly disappeared into the brush beyond the rock. "Blossom!" she called. "Blossom, kitty-kitty!"

"Oh, Rags," Savannah complained.

Rochelle looked at her and asked, "What did he do?"

"Well, I'm not sure," Savannah said, "but I imagine he influenced Blossom in some way. That's one of his specialties—to break away like that and run off." When Rags pulled against his leash she slackened up on it and said, "Come on, Rochelle, I think Rags has a bead on Blossom's whereabouts."

The women and the cat pushed through a growth of shrubbery, then stopped on the other side of it and looked around. "I don't see her anywhere," Rochelle said. "Rags, are you sure she's not still in the bushes there?"

"He doesn't seem to think so," Savannah said, looking down at him. "See him sniffing the air? And he's pulling in that direction—toward those houses. Come on, she can't have gone far."

"Unless someone grabbed her," Rochelle said, trotting to keep up with Savannah and Rags. She grumbled, "My goodness, Rags, you can sure run fast for a cat."

Savannah chuckled. "He's a sprinter, but his endurance is in the toilet."

Just then Rochelle pointed. "There! Oh my gosh, that dog has her. No!" she shouted. She ran after the dog crying, "No-no-no! Drop her! Drop her!"

"Rags!" Savannah scolded as he pulled hard against the leash. "Slow down, you're going to hurt yourself." To the dog, she shouted, "Stop! Hey, let her go! Scram!"

Just then they heard a man's voice. "What's the problem, ladies?"

"That dog has our cat!" Savannah shrieked. She continued to run after Rags and Rochelle.

"No worries," the man said, trying to keep up with the women.

Rochelle glanced back at him. "No worries? Are you crazy?" More hysterically, she said, "He has her by the neck. Look, he's dragging her. Blossom!" she screeched.

"He's just taking her home," the man said, now sounding out of breath. "He likes cats. He's always finding cats and taking them home." He pointed. "See, his gate's open again. He'll take her into his yard and drop her at the doorstep. You just watch."

The women ran up to the open gate and stopped. "Look," Rochelle said, trying to catch her breath, "he dropped her. Is she okay? Blossom!" she called. She asked the man, "Will the dog bite?"

The man chuckled. "No, and I'm sure your cat's okay. I've never heard of Sparky hurting a cat.

Now watch this," he suggested. "See, he paws for Miss Miriam to open the door."

Almost instantly, a woman appeared. "Sparky," she groused, "not another cat. We already have enough cats. What am I going to do with you?" she scolded. "You've got to stop getting out, and no more cats! Do you hear me?" The woman kneeled and petted Blossom. She crooned, "What a pretty baby. He sure slobbered all over you, didn't he?" Miriam wiped her hands on her apron, then picked up Blossom and started to carry her into the house when Savannah let go of Rags's leash and allowed him to run into the yard.

"Another cat?" the woman yelped. She looked up and saw the two women and the man at her gate. "Samuel," she called, "are these *your* cats?"

He shook his head. "Not mine, Miriam. They belong to these ladies."

"Oh," she said. "I should have known, since they're leashed." She scowled. "Where did you have them tied up? Sparky doesn't like seeing cats tied up or otherwise confined."

Savannah chuckled. "They weren't tied up. We were taking them for a walk."

"Or they were taking us," Rochelle quipped. She strolled into the yard. "That's Blossom that you're holding, and this is Rags. So your dog collects cats, does he? I thought for sure he was killing Blossom, carrying her by the neck like that."

Miriam shook her head and chuckled. "No. He has a gentle mouth. He's supposed to be a bird dog—they're bred and taught to have a soft mouth so they don't hurt the birds, but he prefers hunting cats." She grimaced. "We have eight now—all cats he has found and brought home."

Savannah petted the dog. "You are quite the hunter, aren't you?" She picked up Rags's leash and checked her watch. "It's after two thirty; I need to get on the road."

Miriam handed Blossom to Rochelle, who cuddled with the cat. "Thank you," Rochelle said. She turned to the man. "And thank you for helping us track her down. I'd be in a world of hurt if I came home without her."

"Want me to close your gate?" Savannah asked as they walked out of the yard.

"I guess," Miriam said, "only Sparky will just open it again."

The two women gazed at Miriam and Sparky for a moment before securing the gate as best they could. They carried the cats down the pathway and through the azalea bushes to the expansive grassy area, where Savannah lowered Rags to the ground, saying, "Why don't you walk or run if you want to? You'll be in the car for three long hours. Let's use up your energy while we're here, okay?" When he pulled her off balance, however, the leash slipped from her hand, and she grumbled, "Not another lizard. Darn it, Rags. Come back here, Rags! Rags!"

But the cat was not about to change his course. He seemed to be focused on something.

"Where's he going?" Rochelle asked. She pointed. "The lizard's in *that* bush. That's where Blossom wants to go—to see the lizard again. Did Rags not get the memo? Hey, Rags, he's over here!" she called.

Savannah sighed in frustration and trotted after Rags. *Now where did he disappear to?* she wondered, continuing in the direction she'd seen him go. She slowed her pace and glanced around, but Rags was nowhere to be seen. *Did he go out that gate? Gads, that's a road coming into the park, probably used by their maintenance crew. Shoot, I don't need him getting in the line of traffic.* She rounded a curve through the open gate, and that's when she heard it. Growling. She stopped and listened. *Is that a wild animal? I'd better find Rags and quick.*

Hesitantly, she walked closer to where the sound seemed to be coming from—closer and closer, until she could see that the wild animal was actually her cat. "Rags!" she called, trotting toward him just in time to see a man dash into an overgrowth of shrubs. Rags started to follow him, but Savannah was quick enough to grab the leash. "No you don't," she murmured. She picked up the cat, glanced quickly toward where the man had disappeared, and walked with Rags back through the gate.

I wonder what that was about, she thought. *Who was that guy? A maintenance worker just minding his own business or...*

"What was Rags after?" Rochelle asked when Savannah caught up to her and Blossom.

"I don't know," she said, not wanting to frighten Rochelle. She lowered Rags to the ground, held tightly to the leash, and said, "You know, I'd better get on the road, if you don't mind taking me back to my car." She smiled at Rochelle. "I'm so glad you had time for me today. This has been delightful." She winced and looked down at the cats. "Well, for the most part."

"I know," Rochelle said. "I love our chats. I wish we lived closer and could do this more often."

"But would we?" Savannah asked.

"I know what you mean. When we get together we have quality time, whereas if we had the option of seeing each other whenever we could, would we—or would we put it off, you know, sort of take our friendship and close proximity for granted? Yeah, this is probably the best-case scenario—occasional, but meaningful visits." Rochelle suddenly shivered and glanced around.

"What's wrong?" Savannah asked.

Rochelle shrugged. "Oh, nothing, I guess. Just a chill."

Savannah gazed at her for a moment, then tugged on Rags's leash. "Come on, Ragsie, visiting time's over. We need to head back home." When Rags balked, she said, "Don't you want to go home and see Glori and Buffy and Peaches? You surely want to see Peaches and your sister and brother."

"Sister and brother?" Rochelle repeated, amused.

Savannah smiled. "Lily and Teddy." She swooned. "How I miss my children."

"How long have you been gone?" Rochelle asked.

"Long enough that Mom's probably missing me," Savannah quipped. "Yeah, four days."

The women laughed when Rags rolled over onto his back in the grass and looked up at them.

"Come on, lazy boy, you can snooze in the car," Savannah said, picking him up. She looked at Blossom, who sauntered along ahead of Rochelle. "She does real well on her leash. My compliments to Simon."

Rochelle smiled. "I'll tell him. He'll be pleased to hear you said that."

"Actually," Savannah continued, "it's the harness that's the hard part of leash-training, don't you think so? If you can get a cat to tolerate a harness, the leash is a snap." She laughed at her unintentional pun.

Rochelle grinned and agreed. "Yes, that was Simon's most challenging task with Blossom.

Minnie, not so much. She's a bit more adaptable. That's why we take Blossom out more often trying to get her up to speed with Minnie. You're right, she did pretty well today, except for being carted off by a dog, of all things." She shook her head. "That was bizarre."

"Yes, it was," Savannah said. "Cute dog, though."

Rochelle smiled and said, "I think being with Rags has been helpful in Blossom's training."

Just then, Rochelle yelped and cried, "Oh no! I spoke too soon."

Savannah turned to see Rochelle racing after Blossom, who was running after a squirrel. She chuckled, took out her phone, and began filming the scene, saying to Rags, "She's going to kill me." She tucked her phone back into her fanny pack and watched, wondering if she should try to help Rochelle catch Blossom, but realized that two people and another cat might just make Blossom more skittish and stubborn.

"Blossom!" Rochelle called. When she saw the squirrel leap up into a tree and scurry out of reach, she shouted, "No, Blossom! No! No climbing the tree! That's a good girl," she crooned, running up to the cat and grabbing the leash as Blossom stretched as far as she could reach up the tree trunk. Rochelle quickly picked her up and walked slowly back to others, snuggling and crooning to the cat along the way. "That's a good girl. Now we're going home where you're safe, okay? You're not used to running around free like that. You stay with Mommy, okay?" When she approached Savannah and Rags, she grimaced. "Simon would disown me if I lost Blossom." She laughed. "Or Minnie or Clayton or Matilda. He loves his critters." She looked into Blossom's face. "Why don't you stop when I tell you to? Look what trouble it got you into when Sparky found you. Yeah, he thought he'd made the catch of the day. Blossom, you need to pay more attention to me."

Savannah chuckled. "I don't think she's listening, Rochelle. All she's thinking about is chasing that lizard or that squirrel." Savannah tickled Blossom's fluffy tummy. "You have no idea how lucky you are that your mom caught up to you. I don't think you'd fare well against that squirrel and his friends."

Both women laughed when Blossom looked directly into Savannah's eyes and meowed.

Savannah ruffled the fur on the cat's head. "You sassy girl. You really wanted that squirrel, didn't you?" She chuckled. "And that doggie really wanted you."

The women were walking back to Rochelle's car with the cats and the picnic basket when Rochelle stopped. She hissed, "Who's that?"

"Rochelle, you really are jumpy," Savannah said. "It's just some guy walking through the parking lot. He's probably going to his car."

"I hope so," Rochelle said, under her breath. "Get into the car quickly, will you?"

"Sure," Savannah said, glimpsing the man. She opened the back passenger door and urged Rags to climb in, then she placed the picnic basket behind the seat. Rochelle lowered Blossom onto the seat from the other side and both women closed the doors. Savannah opened the front passenger door, removed her fanny pack, and dropped it onto the floor. She started to climb into the car when she heard Rochelle shriek, then there was a dull thud. She looked up to see a man holding Rochelle roughly up against the car.

He demanded, "Give me the keys. Give me your car keys!"

Chapter Two

On impulse, Savannah ran around to the other side of the car to help Rochelle, but stopped when she saw the knife. The man waved it at her and barked, "Stay back, lady." To Rochelle he growled, "Where are they?"

"In my pocket," Rochelle said, her voice a mere squeak.

He stepped back and demanded, "Get them."

Rochelle dug nervously in her jacket pocket, while Savannah looked around hoping to see a witness to what was happening. When she realized they were alone in the parking lot and hidden from view of anyone in the park, her heart sank. *I have to find a way to get Rochelle out of this,* she thought. *Oh my gosh, her premonition...is this her premonition playing out? I can't let it happen. I've got to get help.* She took a few steps forward, stopping, however, when the man put the knife against Rochelle's throat.

He snarled. "Stay where you are or your friend gets it."

Savannah stood stock still, except for the trembling, which she couldn't seem to control.

Rochelle pulled the keys from her pocket, and the man grabbed them out of her hand. "Just let us get the cats out of the car and you can have it," Rochelle pleaded.

"Yeah, right," he growled, slipping the knife into a sheath and pocketing the keys. He glanced around, then opened the back passenger door and shoved Rochelle inside. He snarled at Savannah, "Get in."

Savannah hesitated, thinking, *Maybe I can run and get help.* When he pulled out the knife again and threatened Rochelle, Savannah did as he'd ordered, then watched as he climbed into the driver's seat and started the car. *Now what?* she thought, frantically glancing around, trying to decide what to do. *Rochelle's picnic basket. Maybe I can clobber him over the head with it, then he would crash and we could get away.* She reached into the cargo space and put her hand on the basket, when he made a sharp turn and caused her to fall against the door. *Where's he going?* she wondered. *What's he going to do to us? Wait, this is that back road into the park—the service access or whatever. Oh, no, that's the guy Rags was growling at—the one we saw run into the bushes. I'm almost positive it was him. Gads, there's no one around, and he's stopping the car.*

The man jumped out of the car and opened Rochelle's door. "Get out and turn around," he demanded, removing a pair of handcuffs from his pocket.

Savannah watched in horror as he put the handcuffs on Rochelle's wrists and shoved her back inside the car. When Savannah saw him coming toward her, she scooted closer to Rochelle.

He opened her door and sneered at her. "I really didn't want to deal with two of you today, pretty lady. All I want is her, but here you are." He grasped her arm and insisted, "So come out here and turn around."

Savannah looked at the knife, which was in the sheath at his side, then did as he said.

He quickly tied a bandana around her wrists and tested the knot. "Sorry if it's tight; had to improvise because of you," he said, pushing her back into the car. He added, "I only have one set of handcuffs."

Horrified, Savannah glanced behind her and saw the cats both in the cargo space and both of them nonchalantly having a lick bath. *Why is Rags so relaxed?* She wondered. *I can't believe he's letting this happen. But I'm glad he isn't challenging that maniac. I doubt that guy would think twice about using his knife on a cat. Sheesh,* she thought, *maybe I should have taken Rochelle's dream or nightmare more seriously. Okay, well, we're in a pickle now, and I'd better stop worrying and start paying attention. I can't let my guard down. I'll have to stay alert if we're to get out of this awful predicament. First, I'll memorize that man's face and voice. I'll also watch where he's taking us. My phone,* she thought. *I'll have to figure out a way to get it out of my fanny pack, but it's in the front seat. And how can I use it with my hands tied behind my back? Okay,* she thought, *my eyes. I'll be extra alert to the route he takes—watch for landmarks and things. And I'll watch for opportunities to escape.*

What's he doing? Savannah wondered. When she saw him walk around to the other side of the car and tie a bandana around Rochelle's eyes, she thought, *Oh shoot. There goes that idea down the drain.* Just then she felt something under her feet. *What is that? It appears that Rochelle doesn't keep her car as tidy as she did before they adopted Simon. A baseball cap. I'll bet that's Simon's. Maybe if I...* When she saw the man walk around the car toward her with a sleeping mask, she waited until he opened her door, then she lifted the cap with one foot and scooted it out onto the pavement.

"Lean forward," the man instructed, shoving Savannah's head down so he could slip the sleeping mask over her eyes. He glanced around briefly, jumped back into the driver's seat of Rochelle's car, and drove off.

Well, darn it. I can't see a thing, Savannah thought. *Okay, I'll listen to the sounds outside to gather clues. Wait,* she thought. *What if this is a prank? People play tricks on each other sometimes. Rochelle's birthday's coming up. Could Peter have set this up in order to get her to a party place or the airport where he's waiting to take her away to celebrate?* She almost laughed at herself. *Sadly,* she thought, *that man didn't act like he was joking around, and that knife is definitely real. Besides, Rochelle has been uneasy all day. I'll bet this is what her premonition was all about. Who the heck is he? What does he want? Well, he's not going to get away with this—someone will see two women riding in the backseat of a car wearing blindfolds, and they'll know something's wrong.* She slumped in her seat, remembering, *Rochelle has those darn dark tinted windows back here. No one can see into the backseat.*

Savannah had another thought. *Maybe someone did see us at the park—someone walking to their car in the parking lot or walking a dog near that old access road. It's possible. Maybe they'll report what they saw and an astute police officer will spot Rochelle's car and pull that creep over.*

Just then Savannah became aware of a cat. *One of them is on the seat next to me. I think it's Rags. He feels tense. Oops, I'm pretty sure he just jumped into the front seat.*

"Hey," the man shouted, "what do you think you're doing, you mangy cat. Get out of here before I cut you. Scat!" he screamed.

"Rags," Savannah said quietly. "Come here, Rags. Come on, boy," she crooned, hoping like heck he would, for once, pay attention. She relaxed a little when she felt him land on the seat next to her. "Just stay put, Ragsie," she said quietly.

"Shut up back there!" the man bellowed.

Another several minutes went by before Rochelle blurted, "What do you want with us? There's money and credit cards in my purse. Please, just take them and let us go. We won't tell anyone."

The man laughed. "Not today, Rochelle."

"You know me?" she asked, weakly. "Who are you? Why are you doing this?"

"Yeah, Rochelle, I know you. Why am I doing this? Let me count the reasons." More angrily, he said, "You ruined my life."

"What?" Rochelle gasped. "Ruined your life? What do you mean? Who are you?"

"Just an insignificant bleep in your past," he said, "but not anymore. You'll never forget me after this—if you live to keep the memory. I've been planning my revenge for more years than I can count. I've been waiting for just the right moment, and finally I got it." He snickered. "Yes. I finally have my chance to perpetrate the perfect crime. No one will ever find you two—at least not until I've finished. I'll have plenty of time to play my favorite game." When no one spoke, he asked, "Don't you want to know what the game is? Well, I can't wait to tell you, Rochelle. It's called payback. Payback, Rochelle. Now, do you know who I am?"

"No," she said quietly. "I think you're making a huge mistake. I don't know you and I've certainly never done anything to you. You have the wrong person. Just let us go. Take my car and let us go. Please, if you have an ounce of decency, just let us go."

"I don't know who you are?" he repeated, snickering. "I have the wrong person? Is that what you're trying to tell me? Rochelle Siminski," he recited, "married to Peter Whitcomb, no children except a brat you adopted…"

"Stop!" Rochelle shouted. "Who are you?"

"We're here now," he said, turning off the car engine.

"Where?" she asked. "Where are we?"

"Your new home, of course. Your home with me, Rochelle." He chortled. "…for as long as I need you—until I finish playing the game."

"You've kidnapped us," Savannah said. "Do you know the penalty for kidnapping?"

"No, tell me," the man spat. "Like it matters one iota to me. All I want is sweet revenge, and I have it all planned out how I'm going to get it." He opened the left passenger door, took Rochelle's arm, and yanked her out of the car. "Yes, we'll be playing some games together, you and I. Come on, I'll show you to your room." He leaned into the car toward Savannah. "You stay put, lady. I'll be back for you." He stood up and thought out loud, "I have only one room ready." He then said, "No problem. You can room together." His uncouth guffaw was telling as he said, "Two for one. Heck, this may be more fun than I expected." He looked at Savannah. "An audience. Yeah, an audience of one—not a bad idea." He closed the car door and engaged the lock, then roughly guided Rochelle along an uneven pathway. When she tripped, he steadied her and complained, "Oh, come on, you're more coordinated than that. You were a cheerleader, after all."

Who is he? Rochelle wondered, wracking her brain—trying to remember.

Soon, Savannah began to feel uncomfortable. *It's getting hot,* she thought. *What's taking him so long? If he doesn't let me out of here, the cats and I will die. It's becoming more and more stifling in this closed-up car.* She twisted in an attempt to reach the door handle when she heard the door unlock and open.

"Did you think I'd forgotten you?" the man asked. He grasped Savannah's arm and started to pull her out of the car when he thought of something. "The cats. Come here, kitty-cat."

"What are you going to do to them?" Savannah asked, aware that her voice was shaking.

"Nothing," he said. "I sure don't need cats to take care of. That wasn't part of my plan at all. I'm going to take that garbage off them and turn them loose." Seconds later, he said, "Good bye, cat. Go. You're free." More dramatically, he called, "Go cats! Run free like you were born to do."

"No," Savannah said. "They're house pets. Please…"

"Oh stop your whimpering, woman," he said. "Come on, get out. The cats are fine. They'll find food and shelter."

Be safe, Ragsie and Blossom, Savannah thought. *God, please watch over the cats.*

When he heard her choke up, he said, "Oh now, it isn't all that bad. I'm not going to hurt you." He laughed. "Well, not too terribly much, anyway, unless…" Again he laughed. "Never mind, we'll cross that bridge when we come to it. Some things in life just can't be helped, right?"

Savannah couldn't see because of the eye covering, so she listened to the sounds around her. *Machinery,* she thought. *I hear a machine in the distance. A tractor, maybe, far in the distance. Otherwise it's quiet. Too quiet.* She balked and pulled away from the man's grip.

"I told you to behave yourself or else," he said, patting her cheek with the knife. "Remember, I'm in charge. As long as I have this knife, I'm in charge." Sounding more menacing, he said, "Now, unless you want me to mess up that pretty face, you'd better do as I say."

Savannah let out a deep breath and stopped struggling. *I've been in positions like this before,* she thought. *I'll figure a way out. Patience. I just need to be patient.* She walked along with the man, continuing to listen and sense what was around her. *Thirty steps to a set of five deep cement stairs going down, what, into a wine cellar or a basement?* she thought. *Maybe a storm cellar. A door. I hear him unlocking a door.* Once he'd opened the door, he led her inside. *Ugh,* she thought, *dank, musty. Darn, this is unexpected, but this whole stupid thing is unexpected. I wish I knew what that crazed lunatic has in his mind—obviously some vendetta against Rochelle. What could it be? She's one of the nicest, sweetest, kindest, gentlest people I know. I can't imagine... Where is she?* She blurted, "Where's Rochelle?"

"I'm here," Rochelle said from across the room.

Savannah felt the man untie the bandana from around her wrists, and she quickly pushed the blindfold away from her eyes.

"You won't be needing restraints," the man said. "It's secure down here. I've fitted this room for my purposes." He looked at each of the women. "Relax for now. You can believe I'll be back," he said, cackling as he walked out of the room, closing the door behind him.

Savannah looked at Rochelle, who sat on the edge of a small bed that was pushed up against the far wall. She listened intently. "Three locks? There are three sliding locks on that door?"

"That's what it sounded like," Rochelle agreed, "and maybe a padlock."

Savannah glanced around and hissed, "Is there a window?"

"Yeah, there's a window behind that black drape," Rochelle said, "but there's a metal grate over it."

"So we're not totally underground," Savannah remarked, rushing to the window and pulling back the cover.

Rochelle shook her head. "No. I imagine this was originally a root cellar."

Savannah reached a hand through the metal bars. "I don't think it's glass. It's some sort of hard plastic. Even if we could get that grate off there, we probably couldn't break the window out. Hmmm," she muttered. "We can't see much from here, but at least this room isn't entirely underground."

"And that's a plus because?" Rochelle asked.

"I think we have more options for our escape." She turned abruptly and asked. "Do you have your phone?"

Rochelle shook her head. "It was in my purse. You?"

"I tried to climb into the front seat and get it while I waited in the car. Couldn't make it. Who is he?" Savannah asked.

Rochelle shook her head. "I don't have the slightest idea. If I knew who he is and what his deal is maybe I could use my skills to talk him out of whatever he plans to do." She scowled. "Darn, I should have paid more attention to my intuition and just stayed home today."

"But what would have stopped him from finding you there, or at the studio, or the grocery store? From the sounds of it he's been watching you. He has an agenda." More quietly, Savannah said, "and he sure sounds determined to follow through with it."

Rochelle cringed. "Yes, like he's Obsessed—maybe possessed." Breathlessly, she asked, "Where are the cats?"

Savannah winced. "He turned them loose. That idiot removed their leashes and harnesses and turned them loose."

"Will they hang around here?" Rochelle asked. "Do you think they'll stay close because we're here?"

"I sure hope not," Savannah said. "I think they'll be in danger here. I hope they find a kind soul who'll take them in and check to see where they belong. They both have microchips. That could be our saving grace, if only…"

"Yeah," Rochelle said, slumping, "if only whoever they decide to trust will actually go to the trouble of having them checked for a chip."

Savannah sat down on the bed next to Rochelle. "I'm puzzled, but actually kind of pleased by Rags's behavior."

"Why? What did he do?" Rochelle asked.

"Well, I didn't tell you this, but we ran into that guy at the park earlier. Rags had him cornered. He was carrying on something fierce—you know, growling and hissing. I thought the poor guy was one of the gardeners or something, so I picked up Rags and the man scurried off into the brush."

"So he was there watching us?" Rochelle asked.

"Watching you," Savannah corrected. "Rags seemed to sense that he was up to no good. He did not like that guy, but why didn't he react when the creep grabbed us and threw us into the car? That I don't understand, unless…"

"Unless?" Rochelle prompted.

"Well, unless Rags has a plan."

"Oh, come on, Savannah," Rochelle said. "A plan? Cats don't make plans like that—at least not long-term plans using strategy, do they?"

"I wouldn't think a cat is capable of that, but I can tell you it's way out of character for Rags to sit back and take a lick bath while someone he knows and loves is being kidnapped."

***

Late that afternoon Michael Ivey arrived home with his twelve-year-old son.

"Adam!" Lily cried, wrapping her arms around the boy.

"Adam!" Teddy mimicked, running to hug his big brother. "See my new horsie?" the toddler chirped. "I got a new horsie. It's a painting."

"A paint," Lily corrected.

Michael chuckled and scooped up his two younger children. "I missed you guys. Did you have a fun day?"

Lily nodded excitedly. "I went shopping with Auntie and Grammy. I bought a new Barbie. I had…"

Before the five-year-old could continue, Teddy pushed in front of her. "I eat ice cream. I get new horsie."

"And a mighty fine steed it is," Michael said.

"Not a steed, Daddy," Teddy insisted. "A horsie."

"See my new Barbie?" Lily said, holding up the doll.

"Where's her clothes?" Michael asked.

Lily motioned toward where she'd been playing. She giggled. "All over the floor." She picked up a dress, a coat, and a pair of jeans. "Here are her clothes."

"Well, you'd better dress her; it's chilly out this evening," Michael said.

Adam walked into the kitchen and greeted, "Hi, Grammy."

"Adam!" Gladys said, reaching out for a hug. "It's always good to see you. I heard your dad was picking you up after work, so I made one of your favorites for supper."

The boy's eyes lit up. "Tacos with that yellow-and-white melty cheese?"

Gladys shook her head.

"Hamburgers?" When Gladys shook her head again, he said, "Pizza!"

"I'm afraid not. Gosh," she said, "maybe it isn't one of your favorites. You always ask for seconds and sometimes thirds when we have it."

He glanced around the kitchen. When he saw a package of macaroni on the counter he shouted, "Cheesie burger macaroni!"

Gladys smiled and nodded.

"Thank you, Grammy," he said, hugging her again. "You're the best."

"You're welcome," she said, grinning.

"But there will be a salad served with that, right?" Michael asked, joining his mother-in-law and his older son in the kitchen with the younger children.

Gladys nodded.

"And, Adam, you'll eat a big helping of salad," Michael said.

"I will?" the boy asked. He looked around. "Where's Savannah?"

"She went down to San Francisco to help out with a cat colony this week. She should be back…” he looked at his watch, “any time now.” Just then he removed his phone from his pocket, looked at the screen, and said, “It’s Peter. He probably wants to let me know that Savannah’s on her way home.” He glanced at Gladys. “I haven’t been able to get through on her cell. She must have her ringer turned off or something.” He put the phone up to his ear. “Hi, Peter.”

“Michael, have you heard from Savannah this afternoon?” Peter asked.

Michael hesitated, then said, “No, I was just telling Gladys that I haven’t been able to reach her. I expect her home any minute, though. Why? Do you know what time she left your place?”

“No.” Peter hesitated, then said, “Michael, I’m really worried. Rochelle was supposed to be home by three thirty or four to go with Simon and me to exchange some of the clothes he got for Christmas.” He chuckled. “We want to monitor his choices, and I think she’s a better shopper than I am. Anyway, I haven’t heard from her, and Savannah’s car’s still here.” He added, “Oh, and Rochelle isn’t answering her phone, either.”

“What?” Michael shouted. He glanced briefly at Gladys and walked into the living room. He spoke more quietly. “What do you mean? Are you saying they haven’t returned from having lunch—what, five hours ago? Savannah wanted to be home before dark. Do you know where they went for lunch?”

"Rochelle planned to take a picnic to a park. They have the cats with them."

"Your cats?" Michael asked. "That's odd, isn't it?"

"No, Simon has them walking on a leash now, so we've taken them out a few times. I know Rochelle wanted to try taking Blossom today, thinking she'd learn a few things from Rags."

"Yeah, she'll learn a few things, all right," Michael muttered with a hint of sarcasm. He ran his hand through his hair and paced, as he always does when he's worried. He asked, "So you've tried calling Rochelle?"

"She isn't answering," Peter said.

Michael let out a deep sigh. "Good lord, what could have happened? Hey, Peter, what park did they go to, do you know?"

"Yes, it's Rochelle's favorite park. She loves going there for a picnic or just to walk the trails."

"What's the road like," Michael asked, "you know, to and from that park? Is it in the mountains or something?"

"No," Peter said. "Not at all."

"So there's no place where they could have driven off the road where they'd be hidden from view—no ocean cliffs or anything?" Michael asked. "Is it desolate? Could they have had a breakdown and no one has come along to help them?"

"I guess it's possible that they took a drive somewhere like that. I just don't know. Michael, I'm really worried."

"Well, you have me worried too, man."

Just then Simon interrupted. "Dad."

"Just a minute, Son," Peter said, "I'm talking to Michael."

"But Dad," Simon persisted.

When Peter waved him off a second time, the twelve-year-old said, "Dad, it's about Mom and Savannah."

This caught Peter's attention. "Hold on, Michael. What, Simon? Did they tell you they were going someplace else?"

Simon nodded. "Mom was going to drop off something at Diego's house—you know, his parents are the 4-H leaders."

"Michael," Peter said, "they were going to make a stop. Let me see what I can find out about that. I'll call you back."

"Okay, but I'm going to put a few things together in case I need to make a trip down there."

"How fast can you get here? I think we need to call the police, although I don't believe they can do anything about a missing person for twenty-four or forty-eight hours."

"Well, *we* can do something. I can be there in three hours or less. Call me if you hear anything from the girls, will you?"

"Of course I will," Peter agreed.

"Hey, I'm bringing Adam with me," Michael added.

"Good!" Peter said. "I don't like the idea of Simon being alone at a time like this, and we may not want to take the boys—oh, my God, Michael, this is just killing me."

Michael winced, then said, "Stay in touch."

When Michael returned to the kitchen Gladys took one look at him and froze. "What is it, Michael. Is Savannah…"

"We don't know," Michael said. "Adam and I may drive down to San Francisco. If we hear from Savannah in the meantime I'll let you know, but it looks like something's wrong. Peter and I want to find out what it is."

"Is Mommy lost?" Lily asked, wide-eyed.

Michael swallowed hard. "I hope not, punkin."

"Rags can find her," the five-year-old said. She looked around. "Wait, Rags went with Mommy. Daddy, is Rags lost too?"

"I'm sure they're just fine," Michael said, forcing a smile. "Rochelle's car probably broke down someplace where they can't get a signal…"

"What?" Lily asked, scrunching up her face.

Michael sat down next to her. "Mommy's phone might not be working, and that's why she can't call us." He hugged the child. "I'm sure she's just fine. Adam and I are going to go help her, and we'll bring her home. Okay?"

"And Rags?" Lily asked.

"And Rags," he said.

"What does Peter think happened?" Gladys asked.

"He doesn't know," Michael said. He added, "Heck, they're grown women. They may have driven somewhere on a whim and run out of gas or something. Darn it! Why didn't they keep us informed?" He looked at his phone when it rang again and answered quickly. "Anything?" he asked.

"No," Peter said. "Simon told me Rochelle planned to drop something off to his 4-H leader is all. Simon goes to school with their son, Diego. I checked, and the girls were there around noon. They seemed perfectly fine. So, Michael, you're making the trip?"

"Yes. Stay in touch." Michael pocketed his phone and called, "Adam, get your stuff; you're going with me."

"To Simon's?" he asked. "Cool."

"Gladys, what do you think I need to take?" He choked up. "Savannah always helps me pack."

"Phone charger, toiletries, a couple of shirts, and an extra pair of slacks, shoes, socks, and a jacket. Do you have money—I mean cash? I have some if you need it."

"Thank you," he said, hugging her. "You're a treasure. I have enough cash and a credit card."

"Got a flashlight?" Gladys asked several minutes later when Michael returned with a duffle bag. "I've put together some snacks and water bottles. Here, Adam. It's a container of the cheeseburger mac casserole."

"Thank you, Grammy," Adam said. "Mmm, it smells good."

"Michael, will you eat some?" she asked.

He took a few short breaths and said, "Probably not. I'll get something when my stomach settles down." He hugged Gladys and kissed Lily and Teddy, then picked up his duffle bag and jacket. "Let's go, Son."

"Michael," Gladys said, tears in her eyes.

He looked at her and said, "Oh, I'm sorry, Gladys." He hugged her. "Of course I'll stay in touch. Try not to worry."

"I'll quit worrying just as soon as you call and say everything's okay," Gladys promised, wiping at her eyes.

***

Meanwhile, Savannah perched on a straight-back chair facing Rochelle, who sat on the twin bed. "Well, we've checked every nook and cranny in this room and there seems to be no way out." She looked at the door. "From the sounds of it, he has three of those old-style sliding deadbolt locks on that door and maybe padlocks. What's that about? Does he normally keep bears or buffalo down here?" She faced Rochelle. "Do you have any idea where we are?"

Rochelle considered the question. "If I put some thought to it, I might be able to…" She slumped. "Oh, Savannah, I don't know. I don't even know who that man is, how he knows me, and what in the heck he wants." She stood up. "Why is he doing this to us?"

"He obviously has something in his craw," Savannah said. "You're sure you don't know what it is or even who he is? Could it be someone you counseled recently or maybe even years ago—some weirdo who didn't like your advice, maybe?"

"Oh!" Rochelle exclaimed. "Sure that happens—an occasional client doesn't understand the essence of my psychic reading and blames me when something goes wrong in his life, but I've never known anyone to behave this whacky." She angrily pounded her fist into a pillow. "What is he thinking?" She began to pace and wring her hands, stopping at the window. She grasped two of the bars and tugged on them.

Savannah watched as her friend worked off some of her frustrations, then she asked, "So you don't recognize him? Maybe if you could remember what his issues were, you can help him work through them and he'd let us go."

"No," she said. "I sure don't remember him." She faced Savannah. "But I've done a lot of telephone consultations." She let out a long sigh. "I don't know—I just don't know. That's one reason why I backed away from doing readings. As you know, I only rarely do them anymore."

"Because of negative reactions from people?" Savannah asked.

"Well, that certainly can be uncomfortable. It's annoying when someone questions me after I've tried to explain that it's all up to them. I'm only relaying my impressions and visions. Some people just don't understand that I'm simply a messenger. It's up to them to use or discard what I share in a way that makes sense in their circumstance."

She thought for a moment and said, "Occasionally someone will contact me wanting their money back or just to complain because their dream man turned out to be a jerk or the job they took wasn't what they expected or their ninety-five-year-old mother died, anyway. Well, these are people who don't understand that just because they want a different outcome doesn't always mean they will get it. In some cases, no matter how hard you hope or pray for a particular outcome, that isn't going to happen because it isn't part of your life path. That result won't facilitate your personal growth in this life." She plopped down on the bed again and complained, "There's too much lack of understanding among a wide swath of people when it comes to the work I do and how it applies to their life. They want to dabble in the mystical, but maybe for all the wrong reasons."

"So it *could* be a disgruntled client," Savannah suggested.

Rochelle shrugged. "I suppose, but I'm pretty good at reading people, as you know, and I will often provide a different, more grounded, less mystical reading for those I identify as skeptics. Know what I mean?"

Savannah nodded, then said, "But he knows stuff about you. Your maiden name and the fact that you and Peter adopted Simon, and obviously where you live."

"I thought about that," Rochelle said. "He also mentioned knowing that I was a cheerleader."

"He did?" Savannah asked. "Were you?" She grinned. "Actually, I could see that—a popular, pretty girl going out for cheerleader."

"But isn't it fairly easy to find information like that online these days?" Rochelle asked.

"I suppose it is," Savannah said. "Well, think about it some more, Rochelle. Maybe do a meditation."

"And you think that will help us?" Rochelle asked. "How?"

"Oh, well, yeah. I mean, as I said before, if you know who it is and what his issues with you are, you should be able to maybe defuse the situation—you know, talk him out of whatever it is he plans to do—convince him to let us go." She leaned forward and spoke more quietly. "Rochelle, you have a skill, a God-given gift that few people have. If you've ever needed to use it in a life-and-death situation, now would be the time."

Rochelle gazed at Savannah for a moment, then shook her head. "Well, I don't know who that is, but yes, maybe I can go inside and figure it out, after I've quit freaking out." She covered her face with her hands again and asked, "He turned Blossom loose?"

Savannah nodded. "And Rags." She looked at her watch. "Damn! The guys are going to be nervous wrecks. You said you were supposed to go shopping with Peter and Simon?"

Rochelle nodded. She took a ragged breath, then lay down on the bed and closed her eyes.

***

"Feel better?" Savannah asked when Rochelle sat up and blinked about an hour later. "You really had a good meditation, or were you asleep?"

"A little of both, I guess," Rochelle said.

"Anything?" Savannah asked eagerly. "Do you remember that guy?"

Rochelle shook her head. "I don't think so. I had a wild mix of dreams and visions and none of it made much sense." She looked at Savannah. "How are you? Did you get some rest?"

"Yeah," she said, "I actually lay toe to nose with you for a while and closed my eyes. Only…"

"Only?" Rochelle questioned.

"Only, when I opened them, we were still in this nightmare."

"Really?" Rochelle asked, quizzically. "How do you think that will help? I wasn't aware that you do that sort of thing."

"I'm not sure how it would help, but it's worth a try, don't you think so?" Savannah asked. "After all, I do talk to him using mind talk. Only thing is, he doesn't usually respond. It's all me trying to convince him of something that I want him to do." She closed her eyes.

Rochelle watched her for a moment, then took a ragged breath. "I'd say sure, it's worth a try. Tell him to go get help." She lay down on the bed and closed her eyes. "I'll try to get comfortable here and see if I can successfully meditate."

Their attempt was interrupted when they heard sounds at the door. Rochelle sat straight up and Savannah left the chair and moved against the back wall. After hearing three locks disengage, the women watched the door open. They waited for a moment before they saw the man enter, struggling to carry a mattress. He dropped it in the middle of the room, then closed the door and locked it from inside with a key, which he slipped into his sweatpants pocket. He pulled blankets out of a closet and tossed them onto the mattress, muttering, "Since you'll be staying over…" He pointed. "As you can see, you have a private powder room. I'm sorry you didn't bring clothes and personal items with you." He chuckled menacingly. "I should have sent you an invitation so you'd be prepared. Don't worry, though, I have some things you can wear." He looked at the women. "They'll probably be too big for you, but that's okay." He squinted angrily at Rochelle. "Then I'll be able to ridicule you the way you did me."

"What are you talking about?" Rochelle insisted.

"Payback. It's all about payback," he said. He grinned at Savannah. "Actually, I wasn't thrilled to have a third party involved, but you know what? I think it's going to work out spectacularly. Rochelle, your friend here will be able to see you at your weakest and most vulnerable, being made to feel so low and insignificant that you'll want to end it—I'm talking suicide, Rochelle. You made me suicidal. You don't know how close I came to ending it all, but I realized that it would make no difference to you. That's why I decided not to do it. What would be the reward for me? You'd just go on with your life and I'd be dead." He waved a finger at Rochelle and scowled. "I want you to feel that desperate and unhappy."

"I don't know what you're talking about!" Rochelle screamed. "Who are you?"

"Good," the man said, "you're already suffering with fear for your life and fear of the unknown. I'll leave you now. There will be more later. Oh, and I might even bring you something to eat. I sure don't want you to fade away and pass out or something. I want you with all of your faculties sharp so you'll feel every single discomfort you deserve after what you've done to me."

"Wait!" Rochelle called when he turned to walk away.

"Good evening, ladies. Enjoy your stay." He stopped and ogled each of the women, then opened the door and said, "You can be sure I'll be back."

Chapter Three

"I thought you'd never get here," Peter said, opening to door to Michael and Adam later that evening.

"Has something happened?" Michael asked.

"No," Peter said. "I'm just so worried I can hardly stand it." He stepped back. "Come in."

"Where's Simon?" Adam asked quietly.

"In his room," Peter said. "He's been waiting for you, but he may have fallen asleep."

"Thanks," Adam said, walking down the hall and away from the men.

"He goes to bed this early?" Michael questioned. "It's just after eight thirty."

"He's been pretty upset," Peter said. "The kid has himself exhausted." He glanced toward the hallway. "I'm awfully glad you brought Adam." He slumped into an overstuffed chair and said, "Sit." He watched as Michael removed his jacket and sat down on the sofa. "I called the police."

"Yeah?" Michael asked eagerly.

"They said there were a few automobile accidents this afternoon, but nothing involving a car like Rochelle's or two attractive women and two cats. They aren't in any of the hospitals. Mrs. Ramos, the 4-H leader, said they came there, dropped off Simon's stuff, and left. She said everything seemed okay when she saw Rochelle. I even learned what time the gals got to the deli. A worker there remembers seeing the cats looking at her from Rochelle's car when she arrived at work today around twelve thirty."

"So something happened either on their drive to the park, while they were at the park, or on their way back here," Michael said. "How about driving me over there? I want to see the road they took."

"Now?" Peter questioned. "Michael, I agree that we should trace their route, but don't you think we should wait until daylight?"

"No!" he said, standing up and taking long strides across the room. He faced Peter. "Let's at least follow their tracks to the park and back here to see if there's anything out of the ordinary—you know, like a broken guardrail or disturbed bushes where a car might have crashed. I brought my spotlight in case we see anything we want to explore." He asked, "Were you able to file a missing-person's report?"

"Yes," Peter said. "I didn't think they'd take it this soon. Like I said, I thought there was a waiting period, but that's no longer the case, at least in California. So yes, the police are watching for the girls." He added, "You know, they shouldn't be hard to spot with two cats on leash."

"Yeah," Michael said, "if they're out and about. But if they were—you know—out and about, they'd be answering their phone or calling us, for heaven's sake." He picked up his jacket. "Come on, show me the route they most likely took from the deli, will you?"

Peter sucked in a deep breath and let it out, then stood up. "Okay," he agreed. "Let me get a jacket and tell the boys we're leaving."

***

"There!" Michael shouted several minutes later as the men traveled along a two-lane road.

Peter stepped on the brake pedal. "What?"

"Go back," Michael said. "I saw where someone has gone off the road back there. Turn around."

"Where?" Peter asked after making a U-turn. He saw a car approaching from behind and pulled off onto the shoulder to let it pass.

"A little farther," Michael said, "keep going." He then shouted, "There! See that break in the shrubbery?" Michael shined his spotlight in that direction. "Pull over and let me out. I want to look around."

"Michael," Peter said.

"Just pull over," Michael insisted.

"So what did you find?" Peter asked when Michael returned to the car.

"Nothing, darn it," he grumbled. "Someone did go off the road here, but probably not recently. Let's keep looking."

It wasn't long before the men returned to the Whitcombs' home. Peter drove into his driveway, parked, and slumped. "I was sure hoping to see her car parked there where she always parks. Michael, where are they? What has happened?" When Michael took his phone from his pocket, Peter asked, excitedly, "Did you get a call? Is it Savannah?"

Michael shook his head. "No. I have an idea. I'm calling Parker Campbell."

"Who?" Peter asked.

Michael climbed out of the car, put the phone up to his ear, and explained to Peter, "Savannah just spent a few days with her in the city here." He frowned. "It's going to voicemail, but I guess it is a little late to be calling." He left a message. "Hi, Parker, it's Michael Ivey. Hey, I'm wondering if you know where…I mean, if Savannah said anything to you about…" He cleared his throat and took a breath. "I'm sorry, Parker, it's just that Savannah and her friend seem to be missing. Did Savannah say anything to you about any plans she had for after she left you this morning? Did she mention a drive she was going to take, or someone she was meeting? We're going crazy with worry here. Please call. It doesn't matter what time."

Peter watched Michael pocket his phone, then he opened the front door and led the way into the living room. “Hey, what do you say we have a beer and try to get some sleep? I’d like to get an early start tomorrow, and it could be a long day.”

“Yeah, I don’t think either of us will get much sleep tonight,” Michael said.

***

“Oh!” Rochelle shrieked, sitting straight up on the twin bed. She hissed, “What was that?”

“What?” Savannah asked, lifting herself to a sitting position. “Oh no, is he back? Maybe he’s coming to get those dishes. I hope so; I can still smell that horrid stew or whatever that was he brought us for dinner.”

Rochelle stepped gingerly onto the mattress with Savannah and backed against the wall. She chuckled. “No way you can still smell that. We covered it up with a pillow. Anyway, no, I don’t think he’s coming back. I didn’t hear the door unlock.”

“Then what are you doing on my bed? What’s wrong?”

Her voice pinched, Rochelle said, “Rats. I was finally just about asleep when something ran across me.” She whined, “I think it was a rat. Oh, Savannah, just when I thought things couldn’t get any worse…I hate rats.” She shivered. “I just can’t stand the idea of one touching me.”

"Good grief," Savannah said, reaching for the light switch. She looked around and asked, "Which way did it go?"

Rochelle pointed. "That direction—toward the window."

"Great," Savannah complained. She stood on the mattress with Rochelle and gazed around the room. "Oh," she yelped. "Rochelle, look. That's not a rat; it's a cat."

"Blossom?" Rochelle asked weakly.

Savannah shook her head. "No. It's not Blossom and it's not Rags. It's a tortie. Wait! There's another one. Rochelle," she said excitedly, "cats are getting in here. Maybe there's a way out for us—the cats have come to show us a way out."

"They probably came to eat leftovers from that horrid meal that creepy man brought us," Rochelle suggested.

"Could be," Savannah said, "but who cares? Rochelle, we need to find out how they're getting in here. That could be our way out, unless…"

"Unless?" Rochelle questioned.

"Maybe he came in while we were asleep and brought the cats, but why would he do that?"

"I don't think so," Rochelle said. "I'm sure I would have heard him. I don't think I've slept at all tonight, until maybe just before that cat ran across me. But yeah, why would he toss those cats in here like that?"

"Why would he hold us hostage?" Savannah countered. She walked up to the barred window and examined it. "Are they somehow getting in through here?" She kneeled and ran her hands over the wall and the floor. "There must be a cat door or a loose floorboard or something. Rochelle, help me look for an opening."

Rochelle quickly stepped off the mattress and began running her hands along the walls and the floor. She pushed the twin bed aside and suggested, "Maybe they're coming in from under the bed." When she disturbed a cat, she said, "Sorry." She took another look at the cat and removed the pillow from the bowl of stew. "Are you hungry, little one? Come on cats. Kitty-kitty. Come eat."

Savannah watched as two cats strolled curiously toward the bowl, sniffed the contents a couple of time, and began lapping it up. "I hope that stuff's safe to eat," she said, before returning to the task at hand, but she soon gave it up. "Nothing," she said. "There's no possible way you two cats could have come in here except through that door. Dang, if only I had my phone."

Rochelle tilted her head. "Who would you call, and what would you say? We don't have a clue as to where we are or who that man is or anything."

Savannah grinned. "I know someone who talks to cats."

"*You* talk to cats," Rochelle reminded her.

"Yeah, but when I talk to them, I want them to listen to me. Wade actually listens to them. He hears what *they* have to say."

"Now, that would be useful, indeed," Rochelle agreed. She looked at the cats. "Yes, please show us, where did you come from? How did you get in here?" She looked around the room again and suggested, "Savannah, maybe they came in from another room. The cat door or flap might be on an inside wall—they came in from outside into another room, then found their way in here." She jumped to her feet and ran into the closet.

Savannah trotted into the bathroom. After checking all the remaining possibilities they could think of, the women returned to the larger room. "Well, that's crazy," Savannah said, lowering herself onto the mattress. Rochelle sprawled out on the twin bed and covered herself with a blanket.

Propping herself up on one elbow, Savannah asked, "Listen, Rochelle, have you put any more thought into who among your clients might have gone completely bonkers enough to pull something like this? Has anyone come to mind?"

"Not really," Rochelle said.

"Maybe if you talk about some of your more difficult clients or those with outlandish issues—you'll remember this guy. I really believe that if you could figure out who he is and recall what problems he spoke about in your sessions with him, you would be able to talk him out of—you know, whatever he thinks he wants to do to us. If you don't recognize him you probably worked with him by phone. Think hard. Can you recall anyone who…"

"Gosh, I don't know," Rochelle said. "I'm pretty good at releasing the energy of clients—you know, from my body, heart, consciousness, after working with them, especially those with messy problems." She cleared her throat and retracted, "I mean deeply ingrained issues. That's an important practice for a therapist of any kind, as you can imagine."

Savannah nodded. She smiled. "You have a friend."

"A friend?" Rochelle repeated. That's when she became aware that the small tortoiseshell cat had joined her on the bed and curled up next to her. Rochelle ran her hand over the cat's fur. "How nice," she cooed. She lay back against her pillow, closed her eyes, and continued petting the cat, murmuring, "Just let me think." Moments later she raised her head and said, "Most of my more difficult clients, or those with the more complex issues, are women. Unless this is a woman in a man's body, I think they can all be eliminated." She blew out a deep sigh. "So that leaves men. Let's see…Oh!" she yelped. "Two actually come to mind: Owen and Peter."

"Peter?" Savannah repeated.

"Not *my* Peter," Rochelle said. "Peter G.

They don't often give me their last name when we do a phone session." She grinned. "What they don't realize is that I see their full name on their credit card payment information." She chuckled. "Sometimes they give me a fictitious name, or maybe they use someone else's credit card." She took a breath. "Anyway, Owen was afraid he was going to kill someone. He kept waking up each day with the urge to kill someone—it didn't matter who. He was afraid that if he didn't go through with it he'd go crazy. I hope to heck I convinced him not to do it and to resume the intense psychiatric sessions he had been participating in and had quit. I got that he was actually okay—you know, that he wouldn't follow through—but he was driving himself crazy with the thought of it. He was wracked with fear and confusion and guilt. Poor guy."

"Wow!" Savannah said. "What about the other one?"

"Oh, Peter G. He had a serious anger problem. After he was able to admit to me and to himself that he was angry and that the anger seemed to stem from his deep feelings of worthlessness due to his lack of proper or caring parenting, he promised me he'd get into a therapy group or start seeing a psychologist."

"Why not you?" Savannah asked.

"Well, I've never worked as a clinical psychologist or even a behavioral psychologist. I'm more what you'd call a spiritual counselor or therapist. I like to work with people who have lost their way maybe spiritually or emotionally. My goal is to give the client a jumpstart and the tools to keep their motor running. I make a lot of referrals to people in the field of psychology and psychiatry."

"Interesting. Okay, so do you think this guy could be either of those two clients?" Savannah asked.

She shook her head. "I don't know. I just don't know."

"Can't you call on your psychic abilities to find out?" Savannah suggested.

"That's what people don't understand about the mind of a psychic, if that's even the correct description for me," Rochelle said. "When it relates to me, my *powers*, if you will, go right out the window. Likewise when I'm under stress, and believe me I'm just about as stressed as a person can be right now." She slumped. "I'm sorry, Savannah. I'll keep trying." She looked across the room at a large chest of drawers, stood up, and said, "That atrocious piece of furniture keeps calling to me." She chuckled. "So maybe my *powers* have recovered."

Savannah sat up. "Really? I hope so. Yeah, that is an ugly thing, isn't it? What period do you think it's from?"

"The century of poor taste," Rochelle said.

Savannah looked at her and began to laugh. She tried to respond, but her giggles became uncontrollable.

"It wasn't that funny," Rochelle said, attempting to keep from laughing at Savannah.

"I know," Savannah said, continuing to fight against her urge to laugh. "It's hysteria," she said between chortles. "I'm hysterical." She finally calmed herself and asked, "So you say it's calling to you? Why, do you think?"

"I'm not sure," Rochelle said, "but it's the only thing we couldn't move to look behind for a cat door or a loose board or something. Let's try again to move it, shall we?"

Savannah put her hands on the large chest, then she bent over laughing again. "The century of poor taste," she repeated. She stood up and said, "You're right, Rochelle, it's not that funny." Another wave of the giggles washed over her and she asked, "So why can't I stop laughing?"

Rochelle pointed. "There's another cat. Savannah, I'm pretty sure it came from under this thing." Excitedly she said, "Come on, let's move it. This just may be our way out!"

Before the women could scoot the piece of furniture aside, they heard the first of the dreaded releasing of the locks. They quickly turned toward the door, and Rochelle whispered, "Well, that stopped your hysterics."

Savannah nodded and moaned, "Oh, gosh, what does he want now?" She jumped a little. "Hey, did you see that? The cats just flat-out disappeared. I think you're right—they went under that chest of hideousness."

Rochelle chuckled, then controlled herself and stared at the door.

"Still awake, huh?" the man asked, stepping into the room with two large shopping bags. He dropped them, locked the door behind him, then faced the women. "So, do you remember who I am, Rochelle?"

She did not respond.

He grinned at her and asked, "Are we having fun yet? I must say that I'm having more fun than I've had in years. Just the anticipation of our game gives me a buzz like no other. I'm so charged up right now." He dug into one of the bags, pulled out a garment, and tossed it to Rochelle, instructing, "Put this on."

Rochelle looked down at the soft folds of fabric piled on the floor in front of her and took a few steps back.

"Pick it up and put it on!" he demanded. When she refused, he pulled out his knife and shouted, "Pick it up!"

Rochelle leaned over and dutifully picked up the garment, all the while keeping her eye on the knife. She held it up, saying, "It's way too big for me."

"I know it is. It was my grandmother's dress. She wore it in the fifties and sixties. I want to see what you look like in it. Now, go."

"Go?" she asked.

"Yes, go into the bathroom," he insisted. When he saw her relax slightly, he laughed. "Oh, Rochelle, you don't have a clue, do you? I'm not going to put a hand on you—at least not in that way. Yes, I want you to feel frightened and very, very insecure. That's what I want, but you don't have to worry about me—you know, touching you—at least not in *that* way." More quietly, he said, "Although I *should* abuse you in that way, after what you did to me. It's because of you that I can't—I mean, I'm just not interested in women." He glared at her. "Except for you, Rochelle. I have one thing left to accomplish in this lifetime: living my fantasy with you." He stared down at his hands for a moment, contemplating, then he looked up at her and shouted, "Go put it on!"

Rochelle jumped and walked swiftly into the bathroom, returning wearing the tattered, oversized, rayon floral-print dress.

"That's rich!" the man said, laughing. "Oh, do you ever look ridiculous. I wish your friends could see you now." He said to Savannah, "Look at your so-called friend. Doesn't she look awful and stupid and downright appalling?" He pulled out his phone. "In fact, I think I'll put pictures of you all over the internet." He took a few photos, then stared at her. "Oh yes, Rochelle, you look repulsive. I was pretty sure I could make you look that bad." He walked toward her, took her arm, and said into her ear, "How does it feel to be the brunt of ridicule, huh? Do you like it?" He stood back and looked at her again. "Your hair," he said. "It's already kind of messy and tangled, but how about if I fix it even worse." He laughed. "Funny, huh? I'll fix it even worse." She cringed as he began to tousle her hair and knot it, then he stepped back and said, "Look at the camera, ugly Rochelle. You look awful. You look stupid. No one's going to want to play with you, ugly, stupid Rochelle."

"Stop it!" Rochelle shouted. "Why are you doing this?"

"Oh," he said, grinning at her, "you can't take it, huh? You're not so high and mighty and smart and popular now, are you, Rochelle?" He tilted his head and asked, "Do you know who I am now?"

"Owen? Peter? Listen," she said, "I can help you. Stop with this insidious activity now, and let me help you."

"Help me?" the man said, laughing. "I don't think so, Rochelle." He glared at her. "I don't know who you think you are, but you can't repair the damage you perpetrated on me—no way." He chuckled. "Well, actually, I guess you can. You're doing it already. I mean, just look at you. Yeah, I think my cure is being administered right now." He leaned against the large chest of drawers, crossed one foot over the other and laughed out loud.

"Who are you?" Rochelle demanded, fighting hard to control her emotions.

Rather than respond, the man began to applaud. He jumped up and down and shouted, "Goodie! Goodie! It's happening. My plan is working. I'm in charge now, and you're the one suffering. This is great!"

He stared across the room at her for a few more moments as she stood up against the far wall, holding a blanket up under her chin. Finally he said, "Okay, I'll give you a clue. I'm not Owen or Peter, whoever the hell they are. Here's a hint, Rochelle: Meadow Grammar School, Johnson Street Middle School, Washington High School, orchestra, first period English."

Growing angry now, he spat, "Everyone wanted to sit by you. I wanted to, too, but you never invited me. You wouldn't even look at me. I wanted you to look at me—to see me and embrace me, but I wasn't one of the pretty people. I had pimples, braces, glasses. Even in junior high, I wore glasses and handed-down clothes from the giveaway closet at school." He spoke more softly. "I sat next to you in third period until that new kid came to school. He took my place, and I was moved to the front of the class." He shouted, "The front of the class, Rochelle! I couldn't even see you from there."

He grinned. "I could see you from my bedroom window, though, but that's all I could do was see you—watch you."

"Calvin Stanley," Rochelle said quietly.

"Bingo," he said. "Now you remember." He held his hands out, smiled widely, and said, "I don't look so horrible now, do I? I'm a great-looking guy. Too bad I'm damaged—damaged by you, Rochelle!"

She shook her head slowly. "I remember you now, but I certainly don't remember doing anything to you or even being rude to you, Calvin. I didn't know you wanted to be…um…my friend. You never said anything."

"Of course I didn't. I couldn't bear the thought of being rejected. Not being invited to sit with you and Betsy and Brock and Jameson and Roy—that was rejection enough." He dropped his shoulders and shook his head. "All I wanted in my miserable life was to hang out with you and your group—you know, sit at your table for lunch, go to your parties."

"But I didn't know," Rochelle explained. She shook her head. "None of us knew that you wanted…"

"Yeah," he shouted, "you didn't know I was alive!"

"Calvin," Rochelle said more quietly, "I don't recall ever thinking that you were anything but a fellow student—a little shy, maybe, but with the exact same advantages and opportunities as the rest of us. If you'd only asked, or in some way let us know…"

"Oh, baloney," he said. "You don't know what you're talking about. I made myself available. It was obvious that I was interested in being asked to join you, and you all just ignored me. Rochelle, I want you to know that I am not okay, and that's because of you and your friends—mostly you, Rochelle."

He scowled at her, glanced at Savannah, and said, "You know what, you've got me riled. I need to leave now so I don't ruin my plan, but I'll be back, you can bet on that." He started to leave, then turned and pointed at Rochelle. "You might not remember things the way I do, but you weren't in this body and this mind. You don't know how what you said and what you did and didn't do affected me." He looked her up and down. "Yeah, I might not make advances on you, but I just don't know how I can go on as long as you're living. I've put a lot of thought into this, and I've come to the absolute decision that you are the cause of my constant mental pain." He shook a finger at her and snarled, "You will pay for that." Calvin turned on his heels and left the room, leaving the women with the disturbing sound of the three locks engaging, one by one by one.

"Oh my gosh," Rochelle said, jumping off the mattress and rushing to the door. She listened against the door, then faced Savannah. "He's absolutely out of his mind—delusional. He has completely lost touch with reality—the reality that was, anyway. Is it his memory that is failing, or…"

"I think he was obsessed with you, Rochelle, and he maybe carried that obsession through the years until it diseased his thinking," Savannah suggested.

Rochelle sat down on the edge of the bed. "So what are we going to do?"

"Well," Savannah said, "you know a lot about psychology. Can you use some of it on him?"

Rochelle shook her head. "I doubt it. From the sounds of it he's had this twisted revenge plot in his mind for a long time. He's on some sort of a roll now, and I doubt anything I say can change the course of it." She looked at Savannah. "But what is this plan he spoke of?" Her voice pinched, she said, "What does he want to do to me? And how are we going to get out of here before he does it? I mean, it sounds like he wants me—you know—dead."

Savannah stared across the room at her friend, then caught a glimpse of something to her left. "The cats!" she squealed. She jumped to her feet and trotted to the large piece of furniture. "Come on, Rochelle, let's move this thing and see where the cats are coming in. Maybe, just maybe, we can squeeze through there and escape before he comes back."

***

"Are you hungry?" Michael asked when Adam and Simon walked into the kitchen before dawn the following morning.

"Where's Dad?" Simon asked.

"I assume he's still sleeping," Michael said.

"I doubt it." Simon looked out the window into the backyard. "He's feeding the birds. That's *my* job, but when he's worried he can't sit still. He starts doing everyone's chores, except for making breakfast. Do you know how to cook, Mr. Michael?"

"Sure I do," he said, opening the refrigerator. "Good. We have milk." Michael placed the carton on the table, then removed three boxes of cereal from a cupboard, along with bowls. "Oh, here are some tangerines in this basket on the counter. Eat up, boys," he said, trying to sound more cheerful than he felt. "We'll need our strength today."

Adam watched as Michael poured a cup of coffee and took a sip. "Aren't you going to eat, Dad?"

"Yeah, maybe later," Michael said.

"Dad, you didn't eat dinner…"

"I'm okay, Son. I'll eat when I get hungry."

"Cereal, huh?" Peter complained when he returned to the house. "Is that the best you could do, Michael?"

"Yup," Michael said. "Eat up, drink up. We need to get on the road."

"Are we going with you, Dad?" Adam asked.

"I'm leaning toward *yes*," Michael said. "We need all the help we can get to figure out what the hell—I mean heck—happened. So sharpen those senses, boys."

"Where are we going?" Simon asked. "Do we know where to look for Mom and Savannah?"

Michael sat down with his coffee. He watched Peter pour himself a bowl of cereal, then said to Simon, "We've learned that your mom and Savannah dropped off your application and stuff to the 4-H leader. They left there and went to a deli. Someone remembers seeing them and the cats around twelve thirty. Then they were supposed to go to a park to eat lunch. So we want to walk around at the park—you know, looking for clues. You boys can help with that, right?"

Adam and Simon looked at each other and Simon said, "I'm your man, Mr. Michael." He dropped his spoon and pushed away his bowl. "I sure do miss Mom. I definitely want to help find her and Blossom. I'll look really hard for even the smallest clue."

"Do you have binoculars," Adam asked, "and a magnifier glass?"

"I think so," Simon said. "Right, Dad?"

Just then Michael's phone rang. "Hello. Oh yes, hello, Parker. Thank you for returning my call." He glanced at a clock on the wall. "You're up early."

"I'm an early riser. So what happened?" she asked breathlessly. "You said Savannah didn't make it home last night? You knew she was stopping off to have lunch with a friend, right?"

"Yes. They're both missing—the two women and two cats," Michael said.

"Rags?" Parker muttered, disbelieving.

"Yes," Michael said, "and Rochelle's cat. They took the cats to a park where they had a picnic lunch. The police are looking for them, and Peter, Rochelle's husband, and I are going to try retracing their steps in the daylight—you know, to see if they might be stranded somewhere or something." He took a couple of quick breaths. "Parker, I just wondered if Savannah said anything to you about plans to stop off anywhere else before coming home."

"No, Michael. Oh my gosh, this is frightening. No. She was going to visit her friend, then drive home. That's all I know."

"Parker," Michael said more quietly, "did anything unusual happen while she was with you? Did you two meet anyone who threatened her, or did she mention…"

"No, Michael," Parker said. "Nothing like that."

"Did she seem worried about anything?" he asked.

"No. She just missed you and the kids. She was eager to get home. No, Michael, I can't think of anything at all that would put her in danger or that indicated there was a problem—nothing."

"Well, thank you, Parker. Please let us know if you think of anything, will you?"

"I sure will. And keep me posted," Parker said. "Oh my gosh, I can't believe this. I'm so sorry. I'll pray for her and her friend and your families, Michael. Please let me know if I can do anything. Anything at all."

"Will do," Michael said, fighting against a flood of emotion. "Thank you, Parker."

***

"So you think this is the park where they had lunch?" Michael asked as Peter parked his car less than an hour later.

"Yes," Peter said. "What do you think we should be looking for?"

Michael blew out a breath. "Maybe evidence that they were here, and any clues of something happening here. Obviously the drive from the deli to here and the one between your house and here are pretty straightforward. There don't seem to be any potentially dangerous or remote areas along those stretches of road, so the broken-down-car theory is out the window, unless…"

"Unless?" Peter asked.

"Yeah," Simon said from the backseat,

"unless they went somewhere else—like up into the mountains for a drive or to a haunted house."

Peter frowned. "A haunted house? Where did that come from?"

Simon shrugged. "I don't know, my brain, I guess."

Peter stepped out of the car and the others followed.

"Spread out, everyone," Michael suggested. "Check the ground, trash cans…"

"Trees," Adam said. When the others looked at him, he explained, "Cats climb trees. The cats might have climbed a tree and Savannah and Rochelle went up to get them and they can't get down."

"Or they walked too close to a tree and caught their hair in a branch," Simon said. "Look for hair in a branch."

"Yeah, that's the idea," Michael said. "Let's go."

The two boys and the men had been scouring the area for several minutes when Peter motioned for them to join him at a picnic table. "This is probably where they ate," he said.

Michael looked at the sky. "Yeah, by noon this table would be partially in the sun and partially shaded. Just the way Savannah likes it. She likes to have options."

Peter nodded and continued, "I also found packaging, in that trash can over there, from the deli where they picked up lunch." He looked at Simon. "What do you have there, Son?"

Adam answered, "It looks like a game."

"Yeah," Simon said, "see the X's and arrows and pictures?"

"Where did you find that?" Michael asked.

"In a trash can back there," Simon said, pointing across the park.

"Well, that probably belonged to someone else," Michael surmised.

"But this didn't," Adam said, holding out his hand.

"What is that?" Peter asked.

"A piece of a paper plate. Savannah bought these for Rags's food and treats when I was with her one day. She uses them when she takes Rags someplace. Teddy and I picked them out. See, they have cats on them."

Michael took the piece of the plate from Adam. "Yes, I remember these. It looks like some animal got ahold of this and chewed it up. Okay, so it appears they were here, and they ate lunch." He looked around. "Then what happened? What in the hell could have happened?"

"I'm going to call the police sergeant I talked to yesterday," Peter said. "I want to know what they're doing and what they've learned."

"Well?" Michael asked when Peter finished the call.

"Well, nothing," Peter spat. "I'm just so—I don't know what I am—angry, frustrated…" More quietly, he added, "scared."

When Simon leaned against Peter he put his arm around the boy and held him close. He looked at Michael. "What now?"

"What are the police doing?" Michael asked.

"They're keeping an eye out for Rochelle's car and two women who meet their description. The sergeant said that from the pictures we sent, the women will stand out. Someone will find them."

"But what if…" Michael started.

Peter was quick to say, "He warned us against those."

"Those what?" Michael asked.

"The what-ifs. The sergeant said to just stay the course with hope, and they'll get in touch with us if they hear or see anything. Shall we go back to the house?" Peter suggested.

"I suppose," Michael said, resting his arm across Adam's shoulders.

Adam stepped back. "But Dad, I don't think we've checked everywhere."

"That's right," Simon said. "There may be clues somewhere else away from the table. I think we should look around some more."

"Okay, boys," Michael said, glancing at Peter, who nodded.

After a few minutes of searching Simon called, “Dad! Hey Dad, Mr. Michael, we found something!”

“Yeah,” Adam said, “cat fur.”

Michael rolled his eyes at Peter, and the two men walked to where the boys waited.

“I told Simon not to touch it,” Adam said. “It could be a crime scene.”

“Well, let’s hope not,” Michael complained.

“See, Mr. Michael,” Simon said, pointing, “that sure looks like Blossom’s fur.”

Michael moved closer and examined the fur.

“Here’s the magnifier glass,” Adam said, handing it to his dad.

“Yeah, I think you boys are right. That looks like cat fur.”

“And it’s Blossom’s color. I think it’s hers. That’s a good clue, isn’t it, Dad?”

“Well, Simon,” Peter said, “I don’t know what it tells us that we don’t already know.”

“Oh,” Simon said. He looked at Adam.

“Yeah, I see what you mean,” Adam said. “We already know they were here with the cats.” He looked around. “But we didn’t know they came over this far away from the table. Why did they come over here?”

“Yeah, did they fall down in those bushes?” Simon asked, pushing into the shrubs. “Mom, Savannah!” he called.

"Maybe there's a sinkhole out here, and they fell in when they chased Blossom into those bushes," Adam suggested.

The two men looked at each other, and Michael said, "Well, anything's possible. Let's see what else we can find."

"Adam and I are good clue-finders, aren't we, Dad?"

"Indeed, you are," Peter said, squeezing Simon's shoulder. "Rochelle!" he called. "Savannah!"

"A footprint," Adam shouted minutes later. "Look a shoe print right here where we found Blossom's fur."

"Are you sure that's not *your* shoe print?" Michael suggested.

The boys looked at each other and nodded. "Yeah, that might be," Adam said.

Simon ran ahead of the others. "I'm going to see if we can find that same shoe print somewhere else."

After spending another thirty minutes or so searching for something to give them direction or hope, the group slowly walked back to the parking lot. Once they reached Peter's sedan Simon said, "Look at that car, Dad. That guy sure doesn't know how to park, does he?"

"Where?" Peter asked, obviously preoccupied. "Oh, I guess it's the only car out here except for ours. Yeah, bad job of parking, for sure."

Michael started to get into the car, then changed his mind. He mumbled, "I wonder if someone's in trouble there? I'd better go check it out."

"What?" Adam asked, catching up to him. "What are you doing, Dad?"

"Well, I just wondered if someone passed out in there or something, and that's why the car isn't parked properly."

"Yeah," Simon said, trotting to catch up. "Like an old guy had a heart attack while he was parking and he died in there or got murdered."

"Simon," Peter corrected, "that's morbid."

"Well, it happens," Simon said. "I've seen it on those police programs and on the news."

"Okay," Michael said, "you boys stay back and let Peter and me take a look, okay?"

"I want to see a dead guy," Adam said.

More sternly, Michael said, "You boys stay back."

"No one's in there?" Simon asked, walking toward the men when they headed back to Peter's car.

"Yeah, it could just be someone who stopped to use the restroom," Peter suggested.

Simon and Adam ran to the abandoned car and peered through the windows. "It's old," Adam said.

"And messy," Simon added. "Look at all that junk in there. Hey, he must be a cowboy. There's rope and cowboy kerchiefs and…"

"Yeah," Adam said, "there's a fake beard. That's crazy."

"Come on, boys," Michael called.

"Wait," Simon said. "There's a lot to look at."

"Hey," Michael said, "you don't want that guy to see you all over his car when he comes out of the restroom."

"Well, he's been in there for a long time," Adam said. "I saw that car parked right there when we got here."

"You did?" Peter asked.

"Yeah, you didn't notice it?" Simon asked.

"No," Peter said, "I guess I didn't."

Adam looked at Michael, who shook his head.

"Well, how are you going to find clues if you can't even see a big car parked all weird like that?" Simon asked.

"Get in the car, boys," Peter urged. "Let's go, shall we?"

"And leave that poor guy dying of a heart attack in the bathroom?" Adam asked.

"Well, I guess that wouldn't be very nice, would it?" Peter agreed. "Yeah, I'll go check."

"Can I go with you?" Simon asked.

"Stay there," Peter said. "I'll be right back." When he returned he announced, "No one's in there."

Adam started to get into the car, then stopped and said, "Maybe he's passed out somewhere in the park."

"Don't you think we would have seen him?" Michael asked impatiently.

"He's probably hiking," Peter suggested. "They have some great hiking trails leading from this park."

"But…" Simon started.

"Get in the car," Peter said, giving the boy a playful nudge.

"But, Dad," Simon said.

"Just get in the car," Peter said. "We're going home, and…"

"Wait," Michael interrupted.

"What?" Peter said. "Do you need to use the restroom now?"

"No." He faced Peter. "You say there are hiking trails? Peter, what if…"

"The police said no saying 'what-if,'" Adam reminded him.

"Yeah, but," Peter said. He closed his car door, locked it, and said, "Come on, boys, we're going for a hike."

Chapter Four

"Well, that was invigorating and refreshing," Michael said, more than an hour later, "but basically a waste of time, right?"

"I had fun," Adam said.

"Yeah," Simon said. "Me, too. Hiking's fun, but horseback riding with Mom and Savannah is funner, especially when you find baby kittens." He let out a sigh. "I guess Mom didn't take a hike with Blossom."

"If they did go hiking up there with the cats," Adam said, "they didn't leave any clues—no cat fur, no nothing." He looked up at Michael. "Now what, Dad?"

"I don't know," Michael said. "I just don't know. Peter, want to check with that sergeant again?"

"Yeah, I can," Peter pulled out his phone. Moments later, he announced, "Well, an officer saw a couple of cats overnight, but didn't think anything of it, since they seemed to be alone—you know, probably strays."

"Where were they?" Michael asked.

"Not too far from here, actually," Peter said. "Corner of Foster and Fifth." He looked at Michael. "Want to…"

"Yes," Michael said enthusiastically. "When were they spotted?"

"I guess sometime last night or early this morning—it was a nightshift policeman."

"Is that a good clue, Dad?" Adam asked.

"It could be, Son," Michael said.

"That car's still here," Simon said, as they approached the parking lot.

"Yeah, it's old and dirty and junky," Adam said. "I wouldn't come back for it, either."

"Ready?" Peter asked, opening his car door.

"Yeah," Simon said, running around to the other side of the car.

Adam pushed in front of Simon and reached for the door handle, saying, "I want to sit on this side."

"What difference does it make?" Simon asked, pushing Adam back.

The boys scuffled for a moment until Simon tripped over the curb and fell into a shrub. "Darn it, Adam!" he shouted. As he started to stand up he noticed something. "My baseball cap," he muttered.

"What?" Peter said. "You weren't wearing a baseball cap. Come one, boys, let's get in the car."

"But, Dad," Simon said, running to him with the cap. "This is my baseball team cap. Look, Mom put my name in it in case I lost it in the dugout or someone took it from me."

"Where did you get that?" Peter asked.

"In the bushes there. It was in the bushes. Dad, I remember leaving it in Mom's car when we went out to dinner that time. Mom told me to leave it in the car so I wouldn't forget to take it off at the table or accidently leave it in the restaurant."

Peter took the cap from the boy and looked it over.

"That's the best clue yet, isn't it Dad?" Simon said. "Now we know for sure they were here."

Peter nodded and handed the cap back to Simon. "Yes, we do. Good job, Son."

"Yeah," the boy said, "and good luck for me that I found my cap." He walked around to the other side of the car and climbed inside.

After closing his car door and hearing the other three doors slam shut, Peter drove off.

Michael leaned forward in his seat. "Watch for the cats, boys. They could be anywhere around here."

"The cats?" Peter questioned.

"Yes, if we find the cats we may find Savannah and Rochelle."

"Unless they became separated somehow," Peter said.

"There!" Simon shouted. He pointed. "I think I saw a cat. Watch on the sidewalk there between the parked cars." Seconds later, he slumped. "Oh, I guess that's a dog on a leash—a fluffy little dog."

Peter drove slowly up and down the streets between the park and the intersection of Foster and Fifth, and around several blocks within that area, then Michael suggested, "Peter, how about we take the route from the deli to the park again, but more slowly? Boys, keep watching for the cats."

"Should we watch for Rochelle and Savannah, too, Dad?" Adam asked.

"Yes, of course." Michael thought for a moment and added, "I think we should focus more on the cats. If the gals are safe, they would have come home or called. Yeah, focus on finding the cats. They can probably lead us to Savannah and Rochelle."

"What's that?" Simon shouted as Peter drove along the five-mile stretch of road between the park and the turnoff to their tract. "I saw something. Back up, Dad."

"What was it, Simon?" Peter asked, impatiently.

"It could have been a cat, but I hope not. It looked like it was hurt. Pull over, Dad," he insisted. "Turn around and go back about to where that far telephone pole is. See that kind of lumpy thing?"

"In the road?" Peter asked after turning around. "I don't see anything."

"No. It's not on the road. It's in the dirt." Simon squinted into the distance. "Is that a cat? See, I think it's hurt."

"Good lord," Michael said. "Pull over, Peter."

"What is it, Dad?" Adam asked.

"It looks like a cat, all right, with a snake wrapped around it. Stop here, Peter." Michael started to get out, then stopped and asked, "Adam, would you hand me that towel back there?"

"The one we wiped the windows with earlier?" the boy asked.

"Yes," Michael said. "It's the only one back there, right?"

"Need help?" Peter asked.

"I'll help," Simon said.

"No," Michael said. "Wait there for now."

They watched as Michael approached the cat. After examining the snake from a short distance away, he moved closer and put his hands on the cat, holding him down. He then began to uncoil the snake until the cat was free. Before Michael could get a good grip, the cat leaped from his hands and skittered rather awkwardly into the foliage. Michael looked at the snake in his hands and considered what to do, then walked with it to the car.

"A snake," Simon said. "What kind is it? He's cool-looking."

"It's some sort of boa," Michael said. "He sure had a hold of that poor cat. I think we ought to go down the road a ways and turn him loose."

"Look, Dad," Adam said. "The cat's just sitting there watching you. Shall we take him someplace where he's safe?"

"Yeah," Simon said, "then you can let the snake go free here where his friends are."

"What about the cat's friends?" Adam asked.

Peter chuckled. "I doubt the cat has friends. No one came to his rescue, did they? Yeah, Michael, can you get your hands on the cat?" he asked.

Michael pushed the snake toward Peter. "Here, hold onto him, will you? I'll see if I can get the cat."

"Not me," Peter said, pulling back.

Michael laughed. He looked at the boys. "Would either one of you…"

"I'll hold him," Adam said.

"Me, too," Simon said. "He doesn't bite, does he?"

"He's probably capable of biting, yes," Michael said, "but if you hold him correctly…"

Simon stepped back. "Yeah, let Adam do it."

Michael grinned at Simon, handed the snake to Adam, and walked toward the cat. It took a while, but he finally returned with the cat wrapped in the towel. "Turn him loose, Adam," Michael instructed.

"The snake?" Simon asked. "Can I touch him first?"

"You can kiss him if you want to," Michael teased.

"I don't think I want to do that," Simon said, running a couple of fingers along the snake's body. "He's not slimy at all. I thought he'd feel more like a fish."

"Okay, come on boys," Peter said. "Nature study's over." He asked Michael, "What are you going to do with the cat?"

"Well, I hope you know where we can find a cat shelter that will take him. I think he needs a break, and maybe even veterinary care. In fact," he said, "do you think your veterinarian would take him and place him appropriately?" Michael looked down at the cat. "Hopefully he has a chip and can be returned to his people."

"Sure, let's give it a try." Peter started the car and looked at his dashboard clock. "I hope they haven't closed for lunch yet." He asked Michael as he pulled out onto the roadway, "Do you close your clinic for the lunch hour?"

"Occasionally," Michael said, "but it's usually so that we can get some surgeries done."

***

"I'm glad the cat's okay," Adam said, climbing back into the car. "That veterinarian seemed nice. He sure was surprised to find out what happened to that cat."

"Yeah, he said the only boa he knows that live around here wouldn't hurt something as big as a cat," Simon said, "so maybe the snake was someone's pet and it escaped. Mr. Michael, you shouldn't have let the snake go like that if he's lost."

"You're probably right," Michael said. He turned in his seat and looked at the boy. "Do you want to go back and get him? He can sleep in your room tonight while we try to find his owner."

Simon sat back against his seat and shook his head. A few minutes later, he asked, "Are we going home now?"

"Yes," Peter said.

The boy asked, "Is it time for lunch?"

"You're hungry again already?" Michael asked.

"I didn't eat much breakfast," Simon explained. "All we had was cereal."

"That's 'cause that's all Michael knows how to cook," Peter said.

"That's not cooking," Simon countered. "So do we have lunch at home?"

"Sure," Peter said. "We have fixings for ham-and-cheese sandwiches and maybe peanut butter-and-jam sandwiches."

"I'll have one of each," Simon said.

Peter glanced at the boy in the rearview mirror. "You mean you'll *make* yourself one of each."

"I will?" Simon asked. "You'll let me fix my own lunch? Mom doesn't do that. She fixes it for me."

“Well, Mom isn’t here!” Peter spat. He winced, then said, “I’m sorry, Son. I’m just…”

“I know, Dad,” Simon said. “It’s okay.” Once Peter had parked in their driveway, Simon unbuckled his seat belt and opened the car door. “I can probably figure out how to make a sandwich.”

Meanwhile Adam climbed out the other side of the car. He stopped short and shouted, “Dad! It’s Rags. Look! Rags is here, and Blossom!”

“My God,” Michael said, quickly getting out of the car. “Rags!” he called. “Rags!” He glanced around. “Where’s Mom?” He picked up the cat and headed for the front door. “Is she here?”

“It doesn’t look like it,” Peter said, quickly unlocking the door. “Rochelle’s car’s not here, and why would the cats be outside?” He called into the house, “Rochelle! Rochelle, are you here? Savannah?” He slumped. “Just as I thought.” He looked at the cats. “But how did they get here?”

“Dad,” Simon said, holding Blossom in his arms, “Dad, she looks sick. Mr. Michael, you’re a cat doctor. Does she look sick to you?”

“Come on, boys,” Michael said, “let’s take the cats inside and get a look at them, shall we?”

“Yeah,” Adam said “maybe they brought us a clue.”

“Did they bring something?” Simon asked, watching Michael sit down with Rags on his lap and begin to examine him. Simon cradled his cat in his arms. "I wish I could hear what Blossom is thinking like Mom can sometimes."

Peter chuckled. "Yeah, wouldn't that be a useful tool to have right now? Do you think the cats know where the gals are? Do they know what happened?"

"Well, I can tell you this," Michael said, still holding Rags on his lap. "They walked a long distance to get here. His pads are worn and scuffed. See, he's even bleeding a little here."

"Poor Rags," Adam said, hugging the cat. "I'll bet he's hungry."

"And thirsty," Michael said. "Yeah, he doesn't seem to be hurt, just tired and probably sore." He handed Rags to Adam. "Go see if he'll drink some water. Take Blossom too."

"Her feet look really sore too," Simon said. "Look, Mr. Michael."

"Poor thing," Michael said, examining Blossom's paws. He took the cat onto his lap and looked her over. "Yeah, she's dehydrated and sore, but they seem to be okay otherwise." He handed the cat back to Simon. "Go offer her some water, and see if they want something to eat."

"Can we put bandages on her paws?" Simon asked. "I'll go get the bandages."

"Let's get them hydrated and fed first," Michael said. "That's our priority, then we need to clean their paws. We'll put hydrogen peroxide on the wounds and let them rest. You'll need to watch

Blossom carefully over the next few days, Simon, to make sure her paws are healing okay. If not you should take her to her veterinarian." Michael went into the kitchen to get a glass of water, then returned and sat down.

Peter looked across the room at him. "What are you thinking?"

"Huh?" Michael asked. "Oh, I was just wondering where the cats have been—where they came from." He leaned forward. "Peter, the cats might know where the girls are. Gads, but how in the world can we get them to tell us or show us?" When his phone rang, he looked at the screen. "It's Parker Campbell. Hi, Parker."

"Anything?" she asked. "Have you heard anything from Savannah and her friend?"

"No," Michael said, "but the cats came back. They showed up at Peter's and Rochelle's just now."

"Wow!' Parker said. "That's great and pretty amazing—well, depending on where they came from."

"From a distance," Michael said. "Their paws are all roughed up."

"Awww, poor kitties," Parker said. "So they won't tell you what happened?"

"I'm afraid not. You know, Rochelle is our resident psychic. She's the one who could probably have a conversation with the cats, if you believe in that sort of thing, but…"

"Wade!" Parker shouted.

"Wade?" Michael repeated.

"He's intuitive as all get out, especially when it comes to cats," Parker said excitedly. "Do you have his number?"

"I do," Michael said. "I'll call him." He guffawed. "I'm not sure I believe in that stuff, but…" he choked up.

"I know, Michael. Yes, call him. He's not all that good at a distance—you know, not as precise and reliable when the cat isn't right there with him, but it's sure worth a try. As strong-minded as Rags is, Wade may be able to communicate with him. Call him, and let me know what happens."

"I will," Michael promised. "Thank you, Parker."

"What did she say?" Peter asked, petting Minnie when the cat jumped up next to him.

"She suggested I call her brother. He has a way with animals. He's psychic like Rochelle, only with animals."

"Oh?" Peter questioned. "And how will that help?"

"I'm hoping Rags will tell him what happened and where the gals are," Michael said, placing the call. "Wade, hi. It's Michael Ivey."

"Well, Michael, good to hear from you. Did you have a nice Christmas? How's the family?"

"Not great," Michael said. "Yeah, Christmas was wonderful, but we have a bit of a problem. I'm wondering if you can help us out. In fact, Parker suggested I call you."

"Yeah?" Wade said hesitantly.

"Do you have a minute?" Michael asked. "You aren't in the middle of breaking a wild horse or anything, are you?"

Wade chuckled. "No. I just turned a couple of horses loose in the workout corral. We have folks coming in for a dude-ranch experience tomorrow and I want to have these mares ready to greet them—you know, without too much energy. So what's up?"

"Well, Savannah and her friend Rochelle are missing." Michael let out a deep breath. "Savannah was with Parker, you know, in San Francisco. She left Parker's yesterday to come home, but first she stopped at our friends' home up here near the city, and the two gals went out to lunch. They bought deli sandwiches and went to a park to eat. We've pretty much established that, but they didn't return home, and we're just about worried sick."

"I'm so sorry to hear that, Michael. You must be going crazy with worry." Wade paused then asked, "How can I help?"

"Well, they had two cats with them, Rags and one of Rochelle's cats…"

"And they're missing too?" Wade asked.

"They were, but they just showed up at Rochelle's home. Parker thought maybe you could ask the cats where the gals are, if they even know."

Wade exclaimed, “Wow!” He was quiet for a moment, then said, “Oh my goodness. Yes, Rags has stories to tell, but they’re all sort of a jumble.” He sighed. “That’s how it usually is when I try telepathy at a distance with animals—especially cats. Close up, I can often get them to focus—but at a distance it’s difficult for me.” He said, “Give me a moment, will you?”

“Absolutely,” Michael said.

Finally, Wade said quietly, “Michael, I think someone is holding them against their will. Oh my gosh, they’ve been kidnapped.” He paused. “They’re being held in a big house that’s sort of all alone with no other houses around. What I’m seeing is definitely not a city street. It’s remote and—dang, it appears to be practically falling down—maybe even condemned, but there’s life around it. I get that there are…um…cats—oh yes, cats.”

“What?” Michael asked. “Who? Why?”

“I don’t think I’m going to get that kind of information from Rags, Michael.” Wade was quiet again, then said, “I get that it’s a man—one man. Rags doesn’t seem able to give me his description. I mean, I’m surprised I got what I got from him. Good boy, Rags.” Wade then said, “Those poor cats. Two cats, right? They have been walking for hours. Their paws hurt. You know that, right?”

“Yes, we’re getting them hydrated, then we’ll treat them,” Michael said.

"Good. Hey, Michael, that's all I can get, which is surprisingly a lot compared to the usual. Rags is a good subject, at least today."

"So you can't tell us what the cats encountered on their way home—what route they took or anything that might give us a clue as to where the women are?"

Wade chuckled. "No. Can you imagine a TV screen or computer screen picture all broken up into pixels gone wild?"

"Yeah, I guess," Michael said.

"That's what I get from Rags when I try to tap into their travels from the old house to where they are now," Wade said. "I'm sorry I can't do more."

"Yeah, well that's more than we had before. Thank you so much, Wade, I guess. I mean…"

"I know. Not what you wanted to hear, but it might give you a direction. Michael, I'd advise you to get the police involved. It sounds like Savannah and her friend are in serious danger. Gosh, I'm so sorry."

"Yes, we've called the authorities. We're all out looking for them."

"Good," Wade said. "Please let me know…"

"Definitely," Michael said. "Thank you."

"Thank Rags," Wade said. "And if I think of anything else that might be of value to you, I'll let you know."

"I appreciate it," Michael said, ending the call. He sat with his own thoughts for a few moments, then he began to share, "They've been kidnapped—or at least that's what Rags told Wade."

Peter chuckled. "Michael, if I didn't know Rochelle and hadn't become familiar with that woo-woo stuff she does, I would be poo-pooing the heck out of what you just said to me. But I've become at least a little more open-minded, so tell me more."

"Well, there isn't much to tell—just that it's one man, and he evidently took them to an old abandoned, falling-down house with cats around it. Rags and Blossom made their way home from there somehow. That part wasn't clear to Wade. I mean, we're pretty sure the cats walked a distance by the looks of their paws, but Wade couldn't give us any clue as to their route."

Peter buried his face in his hands, then stood up and shook his head in disbelief. "Kidnapped! Who is it that said not knowing is worse than knowing? I'm so freaking worried about her I'm afraid I'll go crazy."

Just then the boys returned to the living room with the cats. "They ate and they drank," Simon said. "Rags drank the most, but Blossom ate the most. Can we heal their paws now?"

"Yes, bring me some cotton balls and hydrogen peroxide, will you?" Michael suggested. He took the boys into the kitchen and guided them in cleaning and treating the cats' paws, then said, "Good job, guys. Now let's let them rest if they want to." He watched as Simon lowered Blossom into a cat bed, but she immediately jumped out, and climbed into a bed with her sister, Minnie, who licked Blossom's face energetically.

"I'll just hold Rags on my lap," Adam said, sitting down with him. Rags immediately stepped off Adam's lap, and stretched out next to him on the sofa. Adam put one hand on Rags and smiled down at him.

The two men gazed at Rags as well.

"If only the cats could tell us where the gals are," Peter said.

"Where they are," Michael repeated. He perked up. "That's right, they know where the girls are. Rags showed Wade an old house."

Adam asked, "Do you think Rags would take us there?"

Michael shook his head. "I don't know how he could do that. I mean, if they were across the street or around the corner, yes, Rags could walk that short distance, and we could follow him, but it looks as though the cats walked maybe as many as eight miles to get here."

"Eight miles?" Peter questioned. "What makes you say that?"

"Well, that's about the distance a cat can walk in a twenty-four hour period," Michael explained. "But that old house could actually be closer, because cats rarely walk in a straight line—they zigzag and circle all over the place."

"I imagine they do," Peter said, "especially when they don't know where they're going. I mean, how in the heck did they find their way here through neighborhoods and city streets where they've never been before?" He faced Michael. "Do you think someone dropped them off here?"

He shook his head. "Not with the injuries we've seen to their paws. No. They made at least a four- or five-mile walk, I'd say, but your hitching-a-ride theory is interesting. I mean, someone might have driven the cats away from where that lowlife is holding the girls, and they found their way home from there. So we still don't know which direction the cats came from, or anything that would help us to find the women, except for a weak description of a house."

Peter slumped in his chair.

"Maybe people saw them," Simon said. He perked up. "Cats can't talk, but people can."

"Are you saying…" Peter started.

"Yeah," Adam said, "we could put up posters and maybe go on TV and ask people if they saw the cats. People can tell us where the cats were when they saw them, and we could follow the map to Savannah and Rochelle."

Michael sat up straighter in his chair, then stood up. "Yes!" he said, giving both Simon and

Adam a high five. "That's brilliant, and it just might work."

"We're going on TV?" Peter asked.

"Maybe just the internet," Michael said, edging his phone out of his pocket and sitting down. "Most communities have their own local networks for all kinds of things—lost pets, getting rid of junk, finding something they want—a horse or gardener or—you know."

"I *do* know," Peter said, excitedly. "Yes, we have at least one of those sites in this area. So you're thinking we could post pictures of the cats and ask people to contact us if they've seen them within the last twenty-four hours?" He stood up and pumped the air with his fist. "Now we're getting somewhere." He tousled Simon's hair and playfully slapped Adam's knee. "Good job, guys." He sat down and took out his phone. "Where are the cats? I want to get a picture of them."

"I got a picture," Simon said, showing it to Peter. "While we were doctoring them."

"Yeah, we don't want to bother the cats now," Adam said. "Dad says they need their rest. Can I see the picture?" he asked.

"Yes," Peter said, when Simon showed the picture to him. "That's a good one. Send it to me, would you?" He gazed at the boys. "You've both been very helpful. I'm impressed."

Simon and Adam grinned at each other.

Simon asked, "Then can we have lunch—I mean, after you post the cats' picture?"

"You haven't fixed yourself a sandwich yet?" Peter asked.

The boy shook his head and quoted, "Animals first, Dad." He frowned. "That memory just made me sad."

"What do you mean?" Peter asked.

"Savannah taught me that when I went riding horses with her and Adam and Mom that time when we found Blossom and Minnie. It made me sad to think that Mom and Savannah are scared or hurt or something."

"I know," Peter said. "Listen, can you boys fix yourself something to eat? I want to call the police sergeant again, and it may take me a few minutes to post to this site."

Simon looked at Adam. "Sure, I guess." He asked, "Do you know how to cook, Adam?"

"Not really," Adam said, "but I can make a sandwich. Come on, I'll show you how."

The men grinned at each other as they watched the boys trot off into the kitchen.

"All done," Peter said several minutes later. He set his phone aside. "I put the cats' picture and our request on two sites." He sighed deeply. "Man, I sure hope someone saw the cats and maybe the women somewhere. Let's hope that crudball didn't take the girls across the state line or…"

"Well, the police have a description of Rochelle's car and the license plate number, right?" Michael asked.

"Yes," Peter said. "The local police as well as those from surrounding communities are keeping an eye out for them." He looked at Michael. "Was that Gladys you were talking to just now?"

Michael nodded. "Yes. Poor thing, she's pretty worried. I told her we're doing everything humanly possible. She isn't sure whether to be pleased that Rags came back or not. I mean, what does it mean?"

"Oh," Peter said, looking down at his phone. "Here's a message from a gal who says she saw the cats."

Michael leaned forward in his chair. "Really? Already? Where?"

Peter slumped. "Oh, I guess it was at the park yesterday." He grumbled, "That won't be much help."

"Unless…" Michael said.

"Unless?" Peter questioned.

"Well, unless that person saw someone bothering the girls," Michael suggested.

He nodded. "Yes. Let's see what she says. It's a gal named Sharon. She was at the park with her grandkids and she says that two pretty ladies let the children pet cats that looked like the cats in the picture we posted. She said that Savannah and Rochelle were still at the park when she left, and she didn't see anything unusual going on." He hesitated, then added, "That was around one fifteen, according to Sharon."

"Well, that's deflating," Michael said.

"Here's another one," Peter announced, excitedly. "This guy said he thought he saw two cats standing on a street corner at Hilton and Carson. Now that's near here. He said it was this morning—yeah, well, they were on their way home then. We need to know where they were late yesterday, right?"

"Yes," Michael said, "and overnight. I want to try to track them overnight."

"Hey, Dad, want me to make you a sandwich?" Simon asked, walking into the living room with a sandwich on a plate. "Look, Adam showed me how to make my own."

Peter shook his head. "No thank you. I don't think so." He asked, "Simon, are you really going to eat that? What do you have on there, anyway?" He lifted the top slice of bread. "Ham, pickles, olives, two kinds of cheese, and what is that?"

"Turkey," Simon said. He lifted the turkey slice and said, "And salami. Want one?"

Peter winced and shook his head.

"Did you get a message?" Adam asked, sitting down and taking a bite of his sandwich.

"Yes, from someone who saw them at the park," Michael said. "So that's not very helpful."

Peter looked at his phone. “Hey, here’s someone who said the cats visited their church last night. A group of ladies were having a meeting and these two cats came in. She was going to take them home and have them checked for chips, but when she was ready to leave the cats were gone.”

“Where?” Michael asked. “Hey, we need a map so we can mark their course. Can we download a map of the area from your computer?”

“Good idea,” Peter said, walking briskly into the hallway.

When he returned, Michael took the map and laid it out on the coffee table in front of him. He asked, “Now, what do we have? Oh, there’s Hilton Street.” He ran his finger along the map until he found Carson, then he drew an X. “Okay,” he said, “now where’s this church?”

Peter studied the map and pointed. “Here. Oh wow, that’s about four miles away.”

Michael nodded. “And they were there, what, around eight or nine last night? Is that what she said?”

Peter nodded.

Michael ran his hand over the route the cats had reportedly taken back to Peter’s home and uttered, “They seem to have come from this direction.” He studied the map for a few more moments, then circled a large area with a finger. “This is the circumference of their travels so far. It doesn’t create a very clear picture, does it?”

"Not yet," Peter said. "It may actually take a while before we get enough information to piece it all together."

"Mr. Michael, Mr. Michael," Simon said, pointing. "Did you see that? Blossom just threw up!"

"What?" Michael asked, gazing at the cat.

"Ick," Simon said. "What is all that ugly stuff she threw up? Do you think she's really sick?"

Peter chuckled. "I imagine that's some of the junk those church ladies fed her when she visited their meeting. The lady who contacted us said they thought the cats were hungry, and the only things they had to feed them were some cream-cheese-and-cherry bars and a pudding cake."

Michael groaned. "Yeah, that certainly could upset a cat's stomach. It would upset mine." He petted Blossom gently, and said, "I think she'll be just fine, but we'll keep an eye on her, okay?"

Simon nodded.

"Want to clean that up?" Peter asked, picking up his phone to see if he had any more messages.

"No," Simon said, emphatically.

"Yeah," Adam said, "what sane person would want to clean up something like that?"

Peter and Michael grinned at each other, and Michael stood up. "Okay, I'll do it."

"Yeah," Adam said, "my dad's used to icky things like that, huh, Dad?"

"Not that it's my favorite aspect of veterinary work," Michael grumbled, "but yes, it's part of the job description." He took a few steps toward the kitchen and said, "Hey, Peter, we'd better eat something if we want to maintain our energy. We could have a busy afternoon."

***

At the same time, Savannah and Rochelle continued to focus on their escape plan. "I hope we have more strength today than we did last night," Rochelle said. "There was no way we could move that stupid chest after that episode last night with that nutcase."

"Yeah, that was brutal," Savannah said. "I thought that after he left we could work on a breakout plan, but I was exhausted, and I think you were too." She asked, "Did you get some good sleep? Are you feeling better?"

Rochelle nodded. "I think so. I really needed the sleep and that shower. Yeah, I feel stronger today and determined." She looked into Savannah's eyes. "How about you; are you okay?" She cringed. "I feel so awful that I got you into this."

"You didn't do anything, Rochelle. Just stop that kind of talk," Savannah insisted. "Yeah, I slept pretty well. I'd sure like a decent meal, though. Where is he getting that so-called food?" She shuddered and glanced at her watch. "It's almost noon. I haven't slept this late in forever." She took a deep breath and walked closer to the large chest. "Are you ready?" she asked, grasping one side of it

"Let's move it away from the wall and see what's behind it."

Before they could give it a good shove, Rochelle stepped back and squealed, "Oh, hi kitty."

"You saw a cat?" Savannah asked. "Where?"

"It just ran across my feet. Ugh," she said, giving the chest a tug. "This thing is beyond heavy."

"It sure is," Savannah said. She stepped back from it. "I wonder what's in there. Hey, maybe if we remove the drawers we could manage it." She walked around to the front of the chest and pulled on the top drawer. "It's stuck. Come help me—you pull one side and I'll pull the other."

"I think it's nailed shut," Rochelle said. She pulled on the middle drawer and couldn't budge it either. "What does he have in here, gold bars, bricks?" She stood back and looked at the chest. "I wonder if we could get behind it and kick it over."

Savannah laughed. "Yeah, that wouldn't get anyone's attention, would it? Anyway, if we could even tip it far enough to fall over, it would probably go right through the floor."

Rochelle brightened. "Then we could crawl out from under the place."

Savannah grinned at her. "I doubt it. I just remembered, we're in some sort of cellar." She stomped her foot. "I think that wood is laid across a cement slab."

"Crumb," Rochelle muttered.

"My sentiments exactly," Savannah said, "only worse." Then she thought of something. "Tools. We need tools—like a crowbar, maybe a hammer, a screwdriver."

Rochelle rolled her eyes. "Where will we get tools? Are you going to levitate to a hardware store?"

Savannah snickered at Rochelle's attempt at humor, then she thought for a moment and said, "We need to be creative." She pushed the mattress off the twin bed. "Look, metal. I wonder if we could remove some of the springs and use pieces of the metal frame as tools."

"Yeah," Rochelle said, "with the right tool, we might be able to pry that grate off the window and break it—you know, break the window." She put her hands on her hips and studied the chest of drawers. "I'd sure like to figure out how to move that thing, though. Our escape route might be right behind there." She pointed. "Oh, look, there's another cat." When they heard one of the locks disengage, she jumped. "Uh-oh, here he comes."

Savannah pushed the mattress back onto the bed frame and sat down. "There go the cats," she said, chuckling. "I'll bet he doesn't even know they can get in here. Heck," she whispered, "he might not even know they're on the property."

"Ready for lunch?" Calvin Stanley asked when he entered the room. He laughed. "It's not what you're accustomed to or what you and your friends ate at school, Rochelle. *You* got to go to the cafeteria. I was relegated to a table in the back of the room where the nerds and misfits ate their sack lunches—cabbage rolls, butter and sugar sandwiches on balloon bread, lima bean spread on crackers…"

Rochelle put her hands on her hips and spat, "You know what, I'm sick and tired of your *poor me* rhetoric. No one told you to sit at that table. It seems to me it was your choice. Did you ever once even try to sit anywhere else? No. I imagine you just meekly shuffled to the back of the room, not because anyone neglected to invite you to sit with them, but because you didn't have the people skills to do anything but follow the other misfits."

Savannah sat wide-eyed, and Calvin stood stunned. He placed two plates on the mattress, pulled water bottles from his pocket and dropped them, then left the room in a hurry.

"Only two locks," Rochelle said. "He just latched two of the locks."

"Boy, you touched a chord with him, didn't you?" Savannah said.

"I guess so," Rochelle agreed, grinning. She winced. "I just hope that doesn't backfire on us." She jumped. "Oh no. No-no, kitty." She laughed. "It didn't take the cats long to return, did it? They're hungry."

"Yes they are, and they're eating our gourmet lunch," Savannah joked. "Darn it. Poor hungry babies." She quickly picked up the plates and handed one to Rochelle.

"Oh, yummy," Rochelle said, sarcastically. She pinched a portion of her sandwich apart to eat, and put the rest of it on the floor for the cats.

Savannah did the same. She also poured water for the cats, saying, "Now, kitty-cats, you can do something for us. That's how it works. We help you out, and you help us out, okay?"

Rochelle smiled. "Yeah, show us the way out, will you?" She then asked, "So, Savannah, how do you envision that we use the bed frame or springs or whatever to escape this…" she shuddered. "…this prison."

Savannah trotted toward the window. She stood to one side and said, "Someone just drove in. Oh, it could be one of those ride-share drivers. Hey, let's try to get his attention. "Hey, over here!" she shouted. "We're prisoners. Call the police, please!"

Rochelle joined her. She jumped up and down, waved her arms, and shouted. Then took off one shoe, reached through the bars with it, and began striking the window. "Over here!" she called. When there was no response, she lowered the shoe to her side. "Shoot. Calvin's getting into the car with that guy and they're driving away."

Savannah asked, "Do you think this room's soundproof?"

"Could be, I guess," Rochelle said. "Darn! Darn! I wish we could have gotten that guy's attention."

Savannah grinned at her.

"What?" Rochelle asked. "Why are you grinning like that?"

"Well, it appears we can make all the noise we want down here without anyone hearing us, and he's gone and won't be bothering us or catching us…"

"Catching us doing what?" Rochelle asked.

"Tearing that chest apart or breaking that window out or whatever we have to do to get out of here," she explained.

"If we can find the tools to do it," Rochelle grumbled.

"Well, let's try, shall we?" Savannah said. She attempted again to move the chest away from the wall. Rochelle took hold of the opposite side and struggled with Savannah to budge it. Savannah leaned against the wall and wedged one foot behind it, catching just the edge of the chest, then let out a sigh of frustration, saying, "Dang, I can't scoot behind there to get enough leverage against it. Hey wait!" she shouted. "Is this thing nailed down? Maybe it isn't heavy, it's just nailed down."

"Nailed?" Rochelle questioned. "To cement?"

Savannah nodded. "Yeah, I think you can put certain types of nails into cement, don't you?" She looked at the chest. "But why?"

"To keep hostages from escaping," Rochelle said, blowing out a long breath.

Savannah dropped to her knees and examined the feet on the chest legs. "It doesn't look like it's nailed down, but it's hard to tell because the wood is so dark and dirty." She stood up. "I want to see if we can use a piece from that bed frame in a way that will help us to move this thing. I think that should be our priority. If that doesn't work, then we'll go to your plan B and try to pry those bars off the window and break out."

"But we don't know how much time we have—how long he'll be gone," Rochelle said.

"That's right, so let's get busy. Come on." Savannah pushed the mattress onto the floor and began examining the bed frame. "Man, it's old," she said. She grinned brightly. "And it's rickety…"

"Tell me about it," Rochelle said. "It wiggles and creaks all night."

"Well, I think I'll be able to remove this leg fairly easily," Savannah said. She glanced around. "What do we have in here that we could shove under the bed to hold it up so he won't notice it's missing a leg?"

Rochelle glanced around the room. "How about that stack of towels? We'll put that corner up against the wall and he won't even notice."

"Good thinking," Savannah said, continuing in her effort to remove the leg from the bed frame.

"Of course," Rochelle said, trotting into the bathroom and returning with the towels. "Our lives depend on our ability to think these things through, right?"

The women had been working on dismantling the bed frame for several minutes when Rochelle hissed, "Hey someone just drove in. Do you think that's him coming back?"

Chapter Five

Michael, Peter, and the boys had been driving around with Rags in the car for more than an hour, hoping he would give them a signal or point out a clue to help them locate the women. When Michael looked at his watch for what seemed like the hundredth time, Peter said, "Buddy, you're going to drive yourself crazy. You look at that watch of yours like every three minutes."

"And *you're* not going crazy?" Michael spat. When he saw the pain on his friend's face, he said, "Sorry, I'm just…"

"I know," Peter mumbled. "What time is it?"

"Three fifty-three," he said, "and we're no closer to knowing something than we were at three fifty-two, or three fifty-one." He let out a sigh, then asked into the backseat, "How are those burgers, boys?"

"Good," Adam said.

"Yeah," Simon said, "better than the sandwich I made."

"What's the cat doing?" Peter asked.

"Watching us eat our burgers," Simon said.

"Dad," Adam said, "he doesn't like that harness you bought him."

Michael looked back at the cat. "What's wrong with it?"

"I don't know, he just keeps scratching where it straps around him," Adam explained.

Michael took a closer look. "Buddy, it might be a little tight. Why don't you loosen it a little? See if that's more comfortable for him." Michael faced front again and muttered, "Savannah always travels with an extra harness and leash for him, but I couldn't find one among her things in her car."

Peter glanced at him. "Maybe she used it." He continued, "Maybe the cat lost or broke the first one and she used the second one, which he evidently lost last night."

Just then Simon leaned forward in his seat and shouted, "The car! Dad, what if…"

"Simon," Peter scolded, "please don't talk with your mouth full."

"Sorry, Dad," the boy said, swallowing quickly. "It's just that…"

"Besides, you were interrupting," Peter said.

Frustrated, the boy said, "But Dad, it's important. It's about the car. I just saw one like it and remembered."

"What car?" Peter asked impatiently.

"The car parked crazy at the park. Maybe it belongs to the bad guy. If there's just one bad guy, he wouldn't be able to drive his car home and take Mom's car, too."

Peter looked at Michael. "My God, Michael, he's right. No one has found Rochelle's car. He must have taken it—yes, that could have been the scuzzball's car." He pulled over to the nearest curb, saying, "I'm calling the sergeant again, and have them check out that car."

He reached behind him and squeezed Simon's leg. "Thanks, Son. That was brilliant."'

"Daaad," the boy said, "you made me spill my lemonade."

"What did they say?" Michael asked when Peter ended the call.

"They're sending someone over to the park right away," Peter reported. "They'll let us know what they find." He frowned down at his phone. "Hey, we have another response to our post." Everyone sat quietly, eagerly waiting to hear the message. "Holy sh…" Peter started. He glanced back at the boys. "I mean, hey, here's someone who thinks they saw the cats clear across town—like, I'd say this is a fifteen-mile drive. What's up with that? Michael, I thought you said a cat can only walk around eight miles in one outing."

"Yeah, but that's as the crow flies. Cats don't have to stay on the beaten path. They can go through neighborhoods, hop over fences and gates, and take alleyways." He turned in his seat to face Peter. "Rags has been known to hitch rides, too."

“Yeah,” Adam said, “Savannah told me that he took a bus ride once to a fish market.” He laughed, then shoved the remainder of his hamburger into the bag and dropped it onto the floor.

“Had enough?” Michael asked, smiling at the boy.

“Yes,” Adam said, “it’s just hard to be hungry when you miss someone so much.” He took a couple of deep breaths in an attempt to stop the rush of tears he felt coming to the surface.

“I know, Son,” Michael said, squeezing the boy’s knee affectionately. He perked up. “We might be closer to finding them than we know.”

“What makes you say that?” Peter asked.

“Well, Simon reminded us of that car, and I think that’s a darn good clue. It very well could belong to that creep. And now we have a report of another sighting of the cats. We’re on a good trajectory, don’t you guys think so?”

“Trajectory?” Simon questioned.

“Direction; course,” Michael explained.

Everyone nodded, but hesitantly.

“Where are we going?” Simon asked when Peter drove back onto the roadway.

“To talk to the woman who saw the cats across town,” Peter said.

“Yay!” Michael cheered. “Let’s hope Rags gets a scent or something.”

"Where are we?" Adam asked, looking out the window.

"I don't know that I've ever been out this way," Peter said. "It's new to me. Is it familiar to you, Simon?"

"Kinda, but I don't know why," he said.

"What's Rags doing?" Michael asked.

"Nothing much," Adam reported.

"He's just licking his paw where he stepped in my ketchup," Simon said.

Michael looked at him. "Rags put his paw in your ketchup?"

"Yes," Simon said. "I think he wanted a french fry."

Peter shook his head. "That crazy cat."

"Blossom and Minnie don't do things like that?" Adam asked. "I saw Minnie lick milk out of your cereal bowl this morning."

"What?" Peter yelped. "My bowl?" He glanced at the boys in the rearview mirror. "Simon, I told you to watch her."

Michael chuckled. "So your cats aren't as well trained as you thought, huh?"

Peter smirked playfully at Michael, then said, "Here we are."

"What is this?" Adam asked. "Does that lady live in a Dumpster?"

Peter chuckled. "No. She takes care of a bunch of cats in this area. This is where she saw

Rags and Blossom." Just then he picked up his phone and announced, "It's the sergeant calling. Hello!" He listened, then slumped and said, "Oh, great. If only we'd…" He listened for a moment, then said, "All right. Thank you for checking on that for us."

"What?" Michael asked.

"The car's gone," Peter said. "You know, the car that was parked all cockeyed at the park. Someone took it."

"Dang," Michael said. "So close yet so far."

Peter stared down at his phone for a moment, then opened his car door. "Well, come on," he said upon seeing a woman traipsing through a large lot dotted with cat houses, tents, and lean-tos. "I'll bet that's her. Let's see what stories she has to tell us." He stepped out of the car and called out, "Hello. Are you Enid?"

"Yes, hello," the woman said. "Peter?"

He nodded. "This is Michael Ivey and his son, Adam, and my son Simon."

"And Mr. Grey," the woman said, acknowledging Rags, who was in Adam's arms.

"He's Rags," Adam corrected.

The woman cocked her head. "Such an odd name for a cat of his caliber."

"His caliber?" Michael questioned.

"Oh yes, he's quite the cat, that one," Enid said. She looked around. "Where's the pretty fluffy girl he was with? I named her Angel Wings."

Simon chuckled. "Her name's Blossom."

Enid nodded. "Yes. That name works." She frowned. "So what were they doing out and about yesterday alone like that?" She faced Peter. "You say you live in the Scarborough Tract East? That's farther than walking distance from here."

"For a cat?" Michael asked.

"For anyone," she retorted.

"Well, Rags has been known to hitch a ride when he gets tired of walking," Michael said.

"Do tell," Enid remarked. "Does he hitchhike or take public transportation?" she asked, bending over in laughter.

"He took a bus to a fish market once," Adam said, wide-eyed.

Enid stared at Adam, then looked down at Rags, who was now rolling around at Adam's feet.

Peter took a breath, "Enid, you said you saw the two cats. Was it here that you saw them?"

"Yes," she said, brightly. "They stopped in for supper. I was pretty sure they weren't strays. They're in too good of shape, but I sensed that they were lost or something like that, and they were hungry."

"This was yesterday?" Michael asked. "What time?"

"Well, that was one of the strange parts. I fed late yesterday, and it was already starting to get dark, so it was around maybe six thirty. I thought they might stay with the colony cats, but not those two. They ate and they ran, but not before…"

"What?" Michael asked.

"Well, it was kind of odd to me. As long as I've been involved with cats—you know, rescuing and caring for this cat colony—I thought I'd seen it all."

Michael sighed and asked, "What did he do?"

"Well, it's hard to explain, but…" She looked suspiciously at Michael and asked, "How do you know it was him who did something out of the ordinary—I mean, rather than Angel Wings?"

"It's his trademark," Michael said. "He's always got something up his sleeve."

"His sleeve," Simon repeated, chuckling.

Enid smiled at the boy, looked down at Rags, and said, "Well, just before leaving, he dove into that shrub right over there and came out with something in his mouth. I thought he'd caught a bug or a lizard," she laughed, "although, there aren't many lizards around here anymore—not with all the feral cats on the prowl." She continued, "Anyway, he drops this thing at my feet. I look down and see that it's like part of a page from a yearbook. At least that's what it looked like to me." She chuckled. "It could have been *my* yearbook—you know, similar hair styles and all. Only there were just two pictures of women. The rest of the page was gone."

"Do you still have it?" Michael asked.

Peter frowned at him. "Why? Why would you be interested in a piece of trash?"

"Because where Rags is concerned, even trash could be evidence or a clue, maybe." He asked again. "Do you still have it?"

"Yes," she said. "He evidently wanted to give it to me. I just put it in my pocket. Let's see, is this the jacket I wore yesterday?" She shoved her hands into her jacket pockets, then her jeans pockets. "Oh, here it is. Yeah, I'm sure that's a yearbook page. See the pretty women, and there's a signature, or a partial signature."

"Let me see that," Peter said, eagerly taking it from the woman. "It's Rochelle," he said, showing it to Michael. He turned it over a time or two. "Yes, someone has written something under her picture. It looks like it says Rochelle. There's the *elle*, and under that is *vin*. He looked down at Rags and asked, "Michael, so you think this is a clue?"

"If Rags found it, it's likely," Michael said. He took it from Peter. "But what does it mean?"

"I'd say someone was infatuated with that woman," Enid said. "See the hearts around her picture?"

"Oh, yes," Peter said. "Oh my gosh. Michael, I know where her yearbooks are; let's go look through them, shall we?" He asked Enid. "Okay if I take this?"

"Absolutely," she said.

Michael glanced around the area and asked, "So Enid, do you know of any abandoned houses on large pieces of property anywhere in this area?"

Enid thought for a moment. "Actually, yes. Several of them. I ride horses and often go adventuring on the less-traveled roads."

"Okay, well, tell me this," Michael said, gaining energy, "are any of those houses maybe one-half to two miles as the cat walks from here, in any direction?"

"I need to think about that," Enid said. "Hey, can I get back to you?"

"Certainly," he said. "Here's my cell phone number, and I think you have Peter's." He smiled at her. "We sure want to thank you for getting in touch with us. You're a good Samaritan, and we appreciate it."

"Hey," she said, "anything to help out a cat."

"You may have done more than that," Peter said. "You might have saved two lives." He put his arm across Simon's shoulders. "Come on, guys."

"Where are we going now?" Simon asked.

"Home, to do some research," Peter said.

***

Rochelle watched as Savannah continued dismantling a section of the twin-bed frame. After a while, she walked to the window. She stepped closer and said, "Hey, look. Someone just drove in." She hissed, "Savannah, that's it! That's the car I saw in my nightmares."

Savannah joined her at the window. "Do you think that's *Calvin*?" she asked using a derogatory tone. "Is that *his* car? Hey!" she said, "I remember seeing that car in the parking lot when he hijacked us. Yeah, that must have been his car. I noticed it was parked weird. I guess he just left it there. The idiot. So you saw it too?"

"Not at the park," Rochelle said, "in my nightmares. That's the car I saw in my nightmares. Yes, that's him. Oh, brother. So he left his car at the park yesterday and hired that driver to take him back to get it. Where's *my* car? Do you see my car out there anywhere?"

Savannah craned to look. "No. He must have hidden it away so no one sees it and gets suspicious. Dang, when's he going to make a mistake?"

Rochelle shook her head. "He isn't the tidiest guy around. In fact, he's kind of a slob, don't you think so?"

"I don't know, this room's not clean, but it's not cluttered with junk, either," Savannah said.

"Look at that pile of junk outside there," Rochelle said, pointing out the window. "See, the breeze is picking up pieces of paper and swirling them all around."

"Yeah," Savannah said. "It looks like he did some shredding, or he sliced up some books or something and piled the trash up out there. The way the breeze is blowing, that stuff's going to be all over the neighborhood soon." She thought for a moment. "I'll bet he plans to burn it. People who live out like this burn their trash."

"I hope he doesn't light it today with that breeze kicking up," Rochelle said.

Just then something caught Savannah's eye. She stepped back so she could get a better view of something on the ground outside the window. "Do you know what that looks like?" she asked. "A page from a high school annual—you know, a yearbook. See the pictures?"

Before Rochelle could get in position to see it, a gust of wind sent it sailing away.

"Oh, well, you didn't miss anything," Savannah said. She frowned. "I just wonder why someone would cut pages out of a yearbook or any other book, for that matter."

"Who knows?" Rochelle said. Feeling a rush of frustration, she stomped away from the window, picked up the piece of bed frame Savannah had been working on, and slammed it down on the bed a couple of times. She then kicked the chest and hit it as hard as she could with the piece of metal, screaming, "Damn! Damn!"

Savannah watched her blow off steam for a moment, then she hissed, "Rochelle! Rochelle, look!"

"What?" she asked, continuing to hack away at the chest.

"Look!" Savannah said. "You found a weak spot in this thing. You put a hole in the side of it. Give me that thing. I want to see if I can break through the back of it." Before she could take a swing at it, however, they heard the locks disengage. She froze in place, tucked the metal piece under the bed, tossed a blanket over the dresser to hide the damage, and moved to where Rochelle stood across the room.

"Good afternoon, my peach," Calvin said cheerily. "I came to inform you that we'll be attending our high school prom this evening. Rochelle, you're my date, and I have brought you your gown. Fix your hair and be ready for me. The music starts in three hours." He walked closer to Rochelle and said more quietly, "Now, if our evening isn't as lovely as I have envisioned it all these years, I'll most likely have to go with my plan B."

"Which is?" Savannah managed.

"Keep out of this," he spat. "In fact, I haven't decided what to do with you while Rochelle and I go to the prom." He faced Rochelle again. "Like I said, if it doesn't go well this evening, I'll have to obliterate you, your friend, and this whole damn house." He looked around. "Yeah, Uncle Edgar's house will have to go in order to hide my secret—*our* secret, Rochelle—and I'll die knowing I have your respect—that I'm finally one of your elite group." He grinned at her before walking out the door. "I cannot wait!"

The women heard the metallic snap of the three bolts lock, then Rochelle sat down hard on the bed. "Oh, Savannah, what am I going to do? What does he expect?" Her voice pinched, she asked, "What shall I do?"

"You're going to put on your big-girl panties and help me find a way out of here. It's now or never, girl. Let's get to work. We have three hours. We should be able to break out by then. Come on, help me."

Rochelle took a deep breath and wiped at her eyes. "Okay. You keep digging into that wood and see if you can get behind that thing. I'll try to make a screwdriver out of a piece of this metal—you know, an edge of it."

"Good idea," Savannah said. She took a step back. "Oh, hello, kitty. Yup, she came right in from behind that chest thing. I just hope their door is large enough for us to fit through."

"If not," Rochelle said more assertively, we can make it bigger with our tools."

***

"Where do you think Rags got that picture of Rochelle?" Peter asked as he drove back to his house that afternoon.

"Good question," Michael said. "He's a hard one to figure out." He shook his head. "How he manages to come up with random things that relate to a situation is beyond me. Wait," he said, facing Peter. "They took Rochelle's car, right? Could he have found that page in Rochelle's car? That makes more sense than anything, since it's a picture of Rochelle."

"I suppose," Peter said, "but why would she be cutting up pages from her high school annuals?"

"Are they missing?" Michael asked.

Peter shrugged. "We'll soon find out."

After sitting with his thoughts for a moment, Michael winced. "I just can't shake the feeling that it's significant somehow—that it's a clue to where the girls are."

"Kevin, Melvin," Simon recited.

"What are you doing back there?" Peter asked.

"Thinking of names that end in V-I-N."

"Calvin," Adam said, "Gavin. I know a kid named Gavin."

"Alvin," Michael added.

"Is that name supposed to be a first name or a last name?" Peter asked. "Well, we're home," he noted, "so let's go find Rochelle's school yearbooks and get to work, shall we?"

It didn't take Peter long to find the annuals on a bookshelf in their office. He handed one to Michael, one to Simon, and he opened the other one. "Siminski," he said. "That was her last name. Rochelle Siminski."

Simon giggled and repeated, "Siminski. That's funny." He sat down next to Adam on the sofa in the living room and opened the book.

"All of these books seem to be intact," Michael said. "It doesn't look like Rochelle vandalized her yearbooks." He shook his head. "So where in the world did Rags find that page?"

Ignoring him, Peter said, "This is her senior yearbook. Which one do you have, Simon?"

He read the date across the front of it.

"That would be her junior year," Peter said, "so Michael, you have her sophomore year."

The four of them sat turning pages for several minutes when Peter said, "Well, here's her senior picture. There are a lot of autographs on the page, but no unusually crazy comments and no one with a first or last name ending in V-I-N."

"Look at the senior boys," Michael suggested. "See what names you find listed there. I'll do the same here. He might have been a year older or younger." Just then his phone chimed. He looked at the screen and said, "It's Parker. Hello, Parker."

"Hi," she said, "how's it going?"

"Well, Rags…" he started.

"I knew it!" she yelped. "He found a clue, didn't he?"

"Well, yes, at least we think so. How did you know?" Michael asked.

"It's Olivia. Michael, she's kind of frenzied this afternoon. Now, she could be feeding off *my* emotions. I've been beside myself with worry, as you can imagine, and maybe she's just nervous because I am. Then I got to thinking that maybe something was happening there, and it isn't me she's reading, but Rags. So is there any news? Have you found or heard anything?"

We put out some feelers over the internet—you know, with the cats' picture—hoping if anyone saw them overnight they'd come forward, and we could maybe trace the cats' steps to where the girls are."

"Brilliant, Michael," Parker said. "What clue did Rags bring home with him?"

"Well, he left it with a woman who manages a cat colony. She contacted us to say that she'd seen the two cats."

"They stopped off for a handout?" Parker asked.

"Something like that," Michael said.

"What was the clue?" Parker asked.

"Rochelle's picture torn from of one of her high school yearbooks," Michael said.

"Wow!" Parker exclaimed. "What do you guys think it means?"

"We're trying to figure that out now," he said. "We're at Peter's and Rochelle's looking through Rochelle's yearbooks."

Parker was quiet for a moment, then she asked, "Michael, may I come over there and be a part of your investigation? I just keep getting the feeling that Olivia and I might be able to help."

"Sure. How soon can you be here?" he asked.

"Well," she admitted, "I'm just about to enter the Scarborough district now. All I need is the address."

"Olivia told you where Peter and Rochelle live?" Michael quipped.

Parker snickered. "No, Savannah did—you know, when she was here yesterday." She hesitated, then said, "Gads, it was just yesterday when she left here? It seems like eons ago."

"Tell me about it," Michael said. He recited the address. "Yes, come on over. We can certainly use all the help we can get. Thank you, Parker, for caring."

"She's coming over here?" Peter asked, after Michael ended the call.

"Yes. She said she's going crazy at home, and she believes she and her cat might be able to help us." He added, "She's an investigative reporter."

"Great!" Peter said.

"How's it going?" Michael asked when Peter seemed to be losing patience with the book he was looking through.

"Not so good," Peter admitted, slamming the book closed. "Maybe he didn't even go to school with her. I never heard her speak of anyone named Alvin or Melvin or…" Peter opened the book again and said, "Hey, here's Arvin Gainsborough."

"Hold that page," Michael suggested.

"Let me look at him," Simon said, standing up and joining his dad.

Michael continued studying his book. "Here's a guy named Marvin and one named Calvin," he said. "They were both in her class. Do you see their pictures among the seniors?" He added, "That's Marvin Beebe and…"

"Calvin Stanley," Peter said. "Stanley," he repeated. "She did tell me once about someone with that name or a name real similar to that. She said she felt sorry for him because of the way his parents treated him. She thought the guy had potential—he was brainy, but his parents wouldn't let him be a kid, so he didn't have social skills. I guess he lived in her neighborhood, and he'd watch the other kids ride their bikes and roller skate from his bedroom window. She said that by high school the kid—Calvin—was pretty angry. She kinda wondered what happened to him. He seemed to come to mind not too long ago when she bought a Calvin Klein sweater. She said it sort of gave her the creeps to wear it." He suddenly became alert, asking, "Is that someone knocking?"

"Probably Parker," Michael said, standing up. "I'll get it." He pulled the door open and greeted her. "Hi. Come in." He reached out and petted Olivia. "Hi there, pretty girl."

"Michael," Parker said, "I'm just sick. I'm so sorry you and your family are going through this."

"Yeah, the only thing keeping us going is hope," Michael said. "Come in and meet the others. Parker, this is Peter Whitcomb."

Peter stood up and shook hands with Parker. "Nice to meet you." He motioned toward the boys. "This is my son, Simon, and…oh, you probably know Adam."

Parker smiled at Simon, then looked at Adam and shook her head. "No, I've heard a lot about this young man, but I haven't met him yet. Nice to see you, Adam and Simon."

"Hi," Adam said. "Your cat looks like Glori. We have a cat like that."

"I know," Parker said. "Olivia met Glori a few weeks ago."

"Oh," Adam said.

When Parker saw Rags leap up onto the sofa with the boys, she greeted him and smoothed the fur over his back, then she asked, "So Peter, Michael, how can I help?"

Before anyone could respond, Adam asked, "Mr. Peter, why didn't Rochelle want to wear the clothes named Calvin, because of that guy she went to school with?"

Just then Rags stepped onto the book that lay across the boys' laps and began to claw at the page.

"No," Adam said, pushing Rags away. "That's rude. This is Rochelle's book."

Michael quickly picked up the cat. "Naughty boy. He looked down at the page and said, "What's wrong with you? You don't usually tear up books and things. That's Glori. She's our shredder."

Simon ran his hand over the page Rags had scratched. "Wow!" he said. Rags clawed this one guy's face all up. There, see him standing with a bunch of the other kids? I guess it was picture day. They're all lined up in a row."

Parker looked more closely at the page. "Who is it he scratched, anyway? Is it someone significant to your investigation?"

Simon looked more closely at the names below the picture and chirped, "You guys aren't going to believe this."

"What?" the others asked.

As if he couldn't believe it himself, he said, "That's Calvin Stanley."

"Calvin Stanley?" Parker asked. "Hey, bring me up to speed, will you?"

Michael chuckled and explained to the others, "Like I said, Parker is an investigative reporter and writer. She doesn't like to be left out of the evidence." He ran his hand over Olivia's fur as she walked past him. "And her cat is her right hand man…er…girl. Olivia is a female Rags." He said to Parker, "Rags may have just confirmed that Calvin

Stanley might be a suspect in the carjacking and kidnapping."

"Oh—wow!" Parker said. "That's someone she went to school with, Peter?"

Peter nodded. No one spoke for several moments, then he said, "Okay, that's enough proof for me. I'm going to call the sergeant."

"And tell him what?" Michael asked.

"Um, that..." Peter started.

"That a cat clawed a picture of a man Rochelle used to go to school with and, because of that we believe he's the kidnapper?" Michael said.

Peter frowned. "I see what you mean. So what do you suggest we do?"

Before Michael could respond, Peter's phone rang. He picked it up. "Hey, it's Enid. Let's see what she has to say, shall we?" He answered, "Hello, Enid. Did you think of something else useful to us?"

"I hope so," she said, "but it's really kind of a lot to relay by phone. Do you have an email address I could send it to? I've typed it all up, so all I have to do is push *send*."

"Yes," Peter said, PeterArtist at PeterWhitcomb dot com. And thank you, Enid, for taking the time to help us out with this."

"Sure. What I did was mark on a map where there are houses in this area that are either abandoned or condemned or at least run-down. I just hope there's something useful there."

“I’m sure there is,” Peter said. “It will at least give us a place to start. “Thank you so much.”

It didn’t take the men long to study the information Enid had sent. They agreed immediately on a plan of action, then Michael picked up the stack of maps and Peter called out, “Grab your jackets, guys and gals and cat.” He looked at Olivia, who lay on the arm of the sofa with her paws crossed. “I guess that should be cats, plural—two cats, right?” When Michael and Parker nodded, he said, “Let’s go see if we can find the girls.”

“We’re taking Rags and Olivia?” Adam asked.

“Yes,” Peter said, “they’re our secret weapons.”

“We have weapons?” Simon asked.

“No,” Michael said, “only Rags, Olivia, and a map.” He tossed Adam’s jacket to him. “Come on now.”

“Cats have weapons,” Simon muttered while putting on his jacket. “They have claws.”

“That they do,” Parker agreed, following after the others with Olivia.

Once they were in the car, Simon asked, “Can Adam and I see the map?”

“Sure,” Michael said, handing a stack of papers to him. He explained, “The top one is a wide view of the area we’re interested in. We’ve put a red

X on the questionable houses. The other pages show close-ups of the houses we want to check out."

Simon spent a little time with the map and the photos of the houses, handing them to Adam as he finished. Parker studied them over the boys' shoulders. Suddenly Simon picked up one of the pictures and looked at it more closely. "Adam," he said, "quick, give me the magnifier." After spending several more seconds with the photo, he said, "Dad. Mr. Michael, that looks like the car."

"The car?" Peter asked as he drove.

"The car that was parked crazy at the park," Simon said more excitedly. "It's parked here by this old house."

Michael reached for the photo. "Let me see that, will you?" He examined the picture, then asked, "Are you sure, Simon? Are you sure that's the car we saw?"

"Almost positively sure," Simon said. "You saw it, Mr. Michael. It looks the same, doesn't it?"

"You saw that car someplace?" Parker asked.

Simon nodded. "At the park where Mom and Savannah went."

"They had a picnic with Rags and Blossom," Adam added. "That's Simon's cat, Blossom—you saw her at Simon's house. We went to that park and looked around."

"Yeah," Simon said, "and we found clues."

"Really?" Parker asked. "Did Rags help you find the clues?"

"No," Adam said. "Rags wasn't home yet. We found the clues ourselves, and we saw that car parked all crooked, and we looked inside it."

"Yeah," Simon said, "no one was inside dead or drunk, and we thought maybe it was the crook's car, because we couldn't find my mom's car." He sat up taller. "I told Dad and Mr. Michael about the car and made them look at it."

"Good job," Parker said. "And you think the car in that Google-map photo is the same car you saw at the park?" The boys nodded and she said, "You two could be on my investigative team any day."

"Are you a policewoman?" Simon asked.

Parker shook her head. "I'm an investigative reporter. I get to work with a lot of police officers and detectives and investigators on interesting cases, then I write about them." She petted Olivia, who lay on her lap with her paws crossed. "Olivia works with me. She's my feline partner."

"Wow!" Adam said, looking at Olivia. "Does she get into trouble like Rags does—you know, get lost, take people's things, be all nosey and all?"

Parker chuckled. "Indeed she does, but she can also be really helpful. She found a lost little boy just a few days ago." When the boys looked at her with wide-eyed anticipation, she added, "Yeah, the day-care provider couldn't find him. The police couldn't find him. But Olivia found him and she stayed with him, keeping him warm and safe until we could rescue them from under the house."

"I wonder if I could teach Blossom or Minnie to do things like that," Simon said. He asked, "Do you think I could?"

"Well," Parker said, "it seems to me that a cat either has the tendency or not. Just like a dog or a horse. Some dogs flunk out of canine police training, or military school. Not all horses can be trained to compete in rodeos or horse racing." When she sensed Simon's disappointment, she added, "But that doesn't diminish the animal's value as a wonderful pet. All cats, dogs, and horses have worth just like all people do."

"And bears and fish and…"

"Certainly," Parker said. "Even bees and butterflies and birds and…"

"Bats," Simon said. "I read that bats are pretty important too."

"That's right," Parker said, smiling.

Adam leaned toward the front seats. "Are we going to this house?" he asked. "The one with the car?"

"Yes," Peter said. "I was going to start at the one closest to home, but yeah, let's go there first. You think that's the same car, huh, Simon?"

"I'm pretty sure," the boy said.

"Okay now, hopefully that car is parked out there today, and we can get a good look at it," Peter said. "If it checks out, we'll get the police involved, unless…"

"Unless?" Michael repeated.

"Yeah, unless we see something that indicates we need to act fast, right?"

"Yeah, I imagine we'd better play it by ear," Michael agreed. "But I don't want the boys in any line of fire."

"Of course, not," Peter said. "Let's get closer and see what we're up against." He shook his head. "I can't believe the cats walked all that distance."

"Dad," Adam said, "Rags is getting—you know, like jumpy."

Michael turned in his seat and looked at the cat. "Antsy?"

"Yes," Adam said, "and nervous. He's nervous about something."

"Peter," Michael said, "I do believe we're on the right track."

Chapter Six

"Are you ready?" Savannah asked when Rochelle came out of the bathroom wearing the awful gown their kidnapper had left for her.

"I guess so, but I'm scared out of my wits. What if…" she started.

"Hey, I've been thinking," Savannah said. "Why can't we overpower him? There are two of us." She held up the piece they'd taken from the bed frame. "We have a weapon."

Rochelle chuckled nervously. "I thought that was a tool."

"Hey, whatever we need it to be, right?" Savannah said. "While he's focusing on you, I can knock him over the head. That ought to be easy. He can't watch both of us at once."

"But what if he takes you someplace else?" Rochelle asked. "He's probably not going to want an audience." She shuddered at the thoughts running wildly through her head.

"Maybe not." Savannah gazed at Rochelle. "Okay then, if he takes me away, you grab the weapon the first chance you get and use it, okay? That's if I'm not here to do it."

"But…" Rochelle started.

"Look, Rochelle," Savannah said, "we'll have to play it by ear from now on. We don't know what he has planned in his warped mind. If I'm here and I have the opportunity, I'll knock him silly, but if he takes me away, you have to do it. Just sneak that thing out from under the bed and whack him with it, okay?"

Rochelle shook her head. "He's probably taking me somewhere else. Remember, he said something about us going to the ball?"

"Okay, that's okay, Rochelle. Then while you're gone with him, I'll keep working on that chest. I think you're right—breaking through the wood to the wall might be the only way we can access the cat door. If it's not big enough for us to get through, we can maybe make it bigger." She snickered. "Heaven knows we haven't gained any weight in here. I should be able to create a space I can fit through."

"What good's that going to do me?" Rochelle asked. "If he takes me away you won't know where I am."

"If I can make it out, I'll come around to the front or the back of the house and find you," she said. "I won't leave without you. Together we should be able to escape."

"We haven't figured out how to escape from him when he comes down here. Why didn't we overpower him when we had the chance before?" Rochelle asked.

"Good question," Savannah said. "I guess we've been putting all of our energy into breaking out. We didn't think of coming up with a plan to disable him." She held up the piece of metal. "Besides, we didn't have this weapon then."

"Disable him?" Rochelle questioned.

"Yes, you know, get that knife away from him and knock him out or something," Savannah said. "Be ready for that to happen tonight."

When they heard the first lock disengage, Savannah quickly shoved the piece of metal under the bed, stood up, and faced the door. Rochelle instinctively grabbed Savannah's arm for support, then she tilted her head and hissed. "I saw a flash. What was that? Is someone out there?"

"A flash?" Savannah questioned.

"Yes, like a reflection. I think someone's coming. I think it was a reflection off a car or something."

Savannah ran to the window and whispered, "Dang, I don't see anything. Maybe it was a reflection off *his* car. See, his car's sitting out there."

"Oh yes, that car," Rochelle grumbled, tears forming in her eyes.

"Hello, my princess," Calvin said, entering the room. "You are lovely, indeed." He placed a small record player on a table, looked at her again, and frowned. "Only I like you better with your hair down. Take it down!" he insisted. Rochelle looked at Savannah and he shouted, "Now, Rochelle! Take it down. Let it flow." He watched as she unwrapped her hair and let it fall around her face. He smiled. "Lovely. Oh yes, just lovely." He plugged in the record player and moved to turn it on, then stopped. He frowned at Savannah. "You're still here? Well, not for long. You come with me." He grasped Savannah's arm and pulled her toward the door.

Savannah glanced back at Rochelle as Calvin shoved her out of the room, then she watched him bolt the door. He took hold of her again and roughly guided her up the cement steps and toward another set of stairs leading to a porch and through a door into the main house.

What the heck? Savannah thought as Calvin, who was dressed in a light blue suit with a black bowtie, yanked and pushed her along an inside corridor past five doors—she counted five doors—and he finally shoved her into a room at the end of the hall.

"I'll deal with you later," he said. He laughed. "Or not." He closed the door and locked it with a padlock, then trotted back down the hall, out of the house and down the two sets of steps where Rochelle waited, every fiber of her body trembling as she watched him walk in and lock the door behind them. "Are you ready for our date?" he asked. He looked around the room. "No!" he said. "No, this isn't right. There you are dressed in your ball gown and I'm in my suit. This is such dismal quarters. How can we have a beautiful evening in a place like this? We need a more suitable ballroom." Giddily, he said, "This is our first prom, after all." He giggled. "Yes, yes. I know just the place."

Rochelle glanced toward where Savannah had hidden the metal weapon and felt a rush of anxiety. *Oh my gosh, he's going to take me out of here. How will I knock him out and get away? Where is Savannah? Oh no, our plan is ruined. Darn it! I guess I'll just have to get creative. Surely I'll find something else to throw at him or hit him with. All I need is an opportunity. Oh,* she thought, *he has turned his back to unlock the door. I'll just...*

Before she could react Calvin Stanley faced her. He picked up the old Victrola and made a sweeping motion for her to slip out through the door ahead of him. Once they were out in the open, he instructed, "Go up those steps. We'll go in that door."

Rochelle walked slowly up the wooden steps to the porch, her eyes darting from side to side as she searched for a way to escape from the deranged tyrant.

"Just go on in the door there," he said, following closely behind her. "This is the kitchen. Walk on ahead there through the dining room and into the ballroom. There now," he said, placing the antique record player on a table.

When Calvin leaned over to plug in the Victrola, Rochelle quickly glanced around for a weapon. She took a few steps toward a vintage lamp just as he stood up.

"Isn't this better?" he asked. More dramatically, he said, "Now we have more space to dance the night away."

Rochelle glanced around the dusty, musty-smelling room. *It's such a shame what has happened here,* she thought. *This was once a beautiful home. The rug is practically worn out. The furniture looks like it's been here collecting dust for decades. And those heavy faded drapes. Even though they're tattered and torn, they're still doing their job. No one can see in through the windows.* She watched as Calvin stacked three records on the player and started the first song.

"I've never attended a prom. Can you believe that?" he asked, reaching for her.

"Yes, I actually can, Calvin," Rochelle said, standing her ground. "And it wasn't because of anything we students did or didn't do. It was your parents—your upbringing. You know that. They wouldn't let you go to the school proms, eat in the cafeteria, play basketball in the cul-de-sac with the rest of us kids. They forbade you to hang out with the neighbor kids, didn't they? They wouldn't let you be a child. In high school they wanted you to concentrate on your studies and music, right? You weren't allowed to go to any school activities outside of academic ones."

"No!" Calvin shouted, turning in place and running his hands through his hair. "No, that isn't right. It was you. I wanted to belong, but you and your friends rejected me. I was always rejected wherever I tried to fit in."

"That's so not true, Calvin," Rochelle insisted. "You were a superb musician. You were brainy—you got straight As. You were part of the elite, smart student clubs and societies. You achieved things none of the rest of us even came close to. And your parents didn't want you to be distracted by frivolous activities. Am I right?"

Calvin glared at her. "But I wanted to be like all the other kids, and you…"

"I had nothing to do with that, Calvin, and you know it." She asked, "Who made you stay in your room and study while the rest of us played outdoors? A couple of us even came to your door once or twice and asked if you could come out and play. We saw you looking out your window, Calvin. We felt sorry for you. Didn't your parents tell you we invited you to play?"

Calvin covered his ears with his hands. "No. No. You're lying. That didn't happen. No!" he screamed. "Don't tell me those lies. It wasn't Mother and Father, it was you, Rochelle. All these years I…" he started.

"You what?" she spat. "You made up lies in your head so you had someone to blame. Calvin, can't you see what that has done to you? It has filled you with hate and regret and a sick yearning for revenge."

He glared at her, then shouted, "No! No! Mother and Father did nothing wrong. No, Rochelle," he said, smoothing his hair, letting out a calming breath, and staring at her. "Don't you see I can't go there? That's not how my mind remembers things. No," he said, reaching for her. "Tonight we dance. You and me, Rochelle, as it should have been years ago—you and me together."

Rochelle cringed as Calvin took her hand and pulled her to him. She gritted her teeth and squeezed her eyes shut.

"Relax," he said into her ear. "You're so stiff." He laughed. "Like the mannequin I used to practice dancing with." He chuckled. "It was actually Mother's dress form. I wanted to be ready should I ever have the courage to invite you to a prom."

I've got to find a way out of here—away from him, Rochelle thought. *I must stay alert and aware.* She gazed around the room hoping to see an appropriate weapon. *I have to knock him out and escape, but what about Savannah? Where is she? I can't do this not knowing where Savannah is. I can't leave her behind.* Suddenly she had an idea. She pulled away from Calvin, grabbed her stomach, and moaned. “Oh my gosh, I think I’m going to be sick. I’m sorry, Calvin, but I feel awful.” She glanced around. “Is there a bathroom here—please, get me to a bathroom.”

Calvin stepped back and huffed a couple of times. He stomped toward the record player and yanked the cord out of the wall. “So much for my dream evening with you. That wasn’t in my plan—a woman who needs to vomit. Well, that’s not going to happen on my suit or on my shoes.” He spat, “How absolutely demoralizing, Rochelle. Can you imagine how that makes me feel?”

“No worse than I feel,” she said, bending over and clutching her stomach. She gagged a couple of times. “Hurry, please,” she said. “Where’s the bathroom?”

Furious now that she had ruined his plan, Calvin Stanley walked swiftly into the dining room. “Come on,” he snarled. “I’m taking you back to your room.”

“Thank you,” she said weakly, following him through the dining room, into the kitchen, out the door, and down the two sets of steps to the cellar.

“There you are, you sniveling brat,” he said, opening the door for her. “And don’t soil that dress, because we may dance again,” he shouted, closing the door and locking it from the outside.

Rochelle sat on the bed and took a deep breath. “Now what?” she asked aloud. “Will he bring Savannah back here? Gosh, I hope he does. I need to see her and make sure she's okay." She reached for the piece of metal they'd removed from the bed frame and held it in her hand. *In case he comes back,* she thought, *I'll be ready for him. He's getting crazier. We've got to get out of here. Only, I don't know where Savannah is. If he comes back, maybe I can knock him out and lock him in here, then I can go look for Savannah. Yeah, that might work.* She sat quietly waiting for him to return. Suddenly she heard it. She sat on the edge of the bed with the weapon camouflaged in the folds of her dress, and listened as the door opened.

"Here's your friend," Calvin said, pushing Savannah into the room. He started to leave, then stopped and said, "Do me a favor, Rochelle, don't die until I'm ready to make you die. Don't rob me of my final wish—my grand finale."

The two women heard him laughing as he locked the bolts and walked away.

"Are you okay" Savannah asked.

Rochelle nodded. "I pretended I was going to throw up so he'd leave me alone."

Savannah raised her eyebrows and complimented. "Good thinking. Yeah, that would turn off even the grimiest creep,"

"Get me out of this dress, will you?" Rochelle begged. Moments later she returned from the bathroom wearing the slacks and sweater she'd worn to the picnic the day before. She had pulled her hair back into a ponytail. She watched as Savannah returned to digging at the large chest of drawers with the tool they'd made, then asked, "Where'd he take you?"

"To a room at the end of a long hallway," Savannah said. She stood up and stretched. "Dang, this is tedious. I just hope we have enough time to get ourselves out of this mess. She grimaced, then asked, "Did he take you someplace, or did you stay here with him?"

"He took me to what was once an elegant living room or sitting room."

"Nice," Savannah said.

Rochelle smirked at her.

"Oh!" Savannah yelped when she felt something rub against her legs.

"What is it?" Rochelle asked.

Savannah chuckled. "One of the cats." She leaned down and ran her hand over the cat's fur. "Oh my gosh," she shrieked upon getting a closer look. "Rags," she said, picking him up. "Rochelle, look, it's Rags."

"Are you sure?" Rochelle asked. "I mean, yeah, it looks like Rags, but how? I mean, are we becoming as delusional as that twisted man?"

"It's definitely Rags," Savannah said. "Do you suppose the cats have been hanging around here waiting for us to come out of this house? But he's wearing a new harness." She looked toward the chest of drawers. "Ragsie, where's Blossom?"

More excitedly, Rochelle moved closer to the chest and called, "Blossom, here kitty-kitty." She ruffled the fur on Rags's head. "Where is she, Rags? Where's my girl? I thought you'd take care of her." She ran to the window and looked out. She was quiet for a moment, then more guardedly she said, "Savannah, someone's out there. I don't see Blossom, but I swear I saw someone run into that thicket in the distance. See it out there?"

Savannah joined Rochelle at the window with Rags in her arms. "You saw someone?" she asked. "Who was it?"

"I don't know," Rochelle said. "They were too quick. I just caught a glimpse."

"Wait," Savannah said. "I think I hear another cat coming in. "Blossom," she chirped. "Blossom, is that you, girl? Come on in." She then said, "Damn, do we really want them in here? I mean, if we can't get out, how are the cats going to get out?"

"Through that hole or whatever it is behind that thing," Rochelle said. She kneeled and called, "Blossom. Come here, kitty-kitty." Suddenly she sat back on her heels and said, "Well, hello. You're not Blossom, but you're sure pretty. Look, Savannah, we have a new visitor. We haven't seen this colorful girl before, have we?"

"No," Savannah said, staring down at the cat. When Rags struggled in her arms, she lowered him to the floor and continued to look at the new cat. "Olivia!" she hissed. She dropped to her knees and began examining the calico. "Olivia, am I seeing things? Is this really you? It must be. I mean, you're wearing a harness."

"Who's Olivia?" Rochelle asked.

"My friend, Parker's cat," Savannah said, disbelieving. She picked up the calico. "Olivia, what in the world!" She trotted to the window and gazed out.

Rochelle joined her. "It'll be dark soon. Do you see Blossom anywhere out there?" She slumped. "Oh, Savannah, I'm so worried about her." She looked at Olivia, who snuggled in Savannah's arms and asked, "She belongs to a friend of yours? Do you think Rags brought her here? Where in the heck did he find her? Do you think he went to her house? Where does she live?" Rochelle looked at Savannah and said, "Wait, isn't Parker the gal you were staying with? Do you think he went back to her house, twenty miles away?"

"I don't know what to think," Savannah said. "I'm completely baffled. I just hope it's all good."

"You hope it's all good?" Rochelle repeated.

"You know, that the cats are here for the right reasons." Savannah gazed at Rochelle for a moment and asked, "Do you think you could use your powers?"

"What?" Rochelle questioned.

"To find out what's going on," Savannah explained. "I sense that something is happening behind the scenes—I mean, with Rags and Olivia showing up. Try, Rochelle," she urged. "Go to your quiet place and see if you can see our future. What's about to happen. I'm sure something's about to happen."

Rochelle gazed at Savannah for a few moments, then stood in front of the window and stared out toward the thicket. She closed her eyes for just a few minutes before hissing, "Savannah. Savannah, you're right. I think they're here—Peter and Michael. They're near. My sense is that they sent Rags in to let us know we're safe."

Savannah stared into her friend's eyes and asked gently, "Rochelle, are you all right? You seem a little hysterical."

Rochelle assured her, "Yes, I'm just fine. In fact, I'm more than all right. Come on, let's get ready to go. They'll be here soon."

Savannah gazed out the window again and saw nothing but pending darkness. "God, Rochelle, I hope you're right."

***

Minutes later, both women lay on the mattress with the two cats waiting for what would come next.

"I'm so exhausted, I could sleep for a week," Rochelle said.

"Yeah, scraping and hacking with that stupid tool thing we made is tedious and tiring," Savannah agreed.

"Not to mention the stress we've endured," Rochelle added.

Savannah propped herself up on one elbow. "What's taking them so long? Rochelle, could you have been wrong about the guys being out there?"

"Sure, I could," Rochelle spat. "It happens." She glared at Savannah. "Are *you* ever wrong?"

Savannah frowned at her, then began laughing.

"What's so blasted funny?" Rochelle asked.

"You," Savannah said. "I don't get to see you ruffled very often. Hey, I'm sorry. I didn't mean to question you in that way. It's just that…"

"I know," Rochelle said, taking a deep breath. She sat up and petted Olivia, who lay next to her. She squeezed the cat to her. "I'm just so…"

Savannah nodded. "I totally understand, and I apologize for questioning you like that." She adjusted Rags's position across her legs. When he suddenly became alert, she jumped and asked, "What's that?"

Rochelle recoiled. "What? Is he coming back?"

"Listen," Savannah said. "Is that someone knocking? Someone's outside there." When Rags leaped to the floor and ran under the chest, she trotted after him. "Hello," she called.

That's when they heard it—a woman's muffled voice: "Savannah Ivey? Rochelle Whitcomb?"

"Who is that?" Rochelle asked, grabbing Savannah's arm.

"It's coming from under that big chest," Savannah said, "where the cats come in. "Hello," she said, again. She moved closer. "We're in here. He has us locked in. Who are you?"

"Officer Rosalind Turner and Sergeant Jim Babcock. Where is he now?" she asked.

"He left us over an hour ago, but he could be returning just about any time," Savannah said.

"To maybe kill us," Rochelle added. "He has a vendetta against me." Her voice pinched, she said, "I think he plans to kill us."

"Are you okay? Has he…" the officer asked.

"We're okay," Savannah said. She moved over in front of the window. "You can see us, right? I'm at the window."

When the officer didn't respond, Rochelle said, "Savannah's in front of the window. Can you see her?"

"No," the officer said. "I see the window, but I can't see through it. It's black."

"Well, now that makes sense," Rochelle said. "No wonder that driver didn't respond to our frantic attempt to get his attention."

"Did you know there's a cat door right outside here?" Officer Turner asked.

"We suspected that, but there's a huge piece of furniture in front of it. It might be nailed to the floor, because we can't budge it. There must be just enough room for the cats to get in and out."

"And the cats are in there with you, right—the big grey-and-white cat and the colorful one?" Officer Turner asked.

"Yes," Savannah said, having returned to where Rochelle crouched near the large chest.

"Okay, well, we'll go get some tools and see if we can break you out of there. Your husbands and your boys are waiting for you."

"Please hurry," Rochelle said, tears flowing down her cheeks. "I'm afraid that guy's a ticking time bomb."

***

"Mr. Whitcomb," Sergeant Babcock said into his phone moments later, "we found them. The cats led us to them. They're okay."

Peter threw his head back and said, "Thank God." To the others he said, "They're okay."

Michael closed his eyes for a moment, then pulled Adam to him and hugged him. When he saw Simon wiping at his eyes, he squeezed the boy's shoulder and smiled down at him. "She's okay, buddy. Your mom's okay."

Simon nodded and fought back tears of relief and joy.

When Michael walked closer to Peter in order to hear his side of the conversation with the sergeant, Parker put her arm across Simon's shoulders and squeezed him to her. She glanced at Adam. "You boys did a great job. If ever I wanted someone on my investigative team, I'd choose the two of you."

At the same time, Peter asked into the phone, "So the cats found them?"

"Yes. We led the cats toward the house on their leashes like Ms. Campbell suggested, and when they showed an interest in going in through what appeared to be a cat door, we took the leashes off them and in they went. The women—your wife and her friend, said there's a heavy piece of furniture maybe nailed down to the floor in front of the cat door, so cats can go in and out, but the women can't get to it." He chuckled. "I guess they've been trying. "Those are some gutsy women in there."

Peter smiled weakly, then asked, "So you know where they are in that big house?"

"Yes. They're in a sort of cellar or basement room on the west side of the house. Tell Mr. Ivey and Ms. Campbell that the cats are with the women inside."

"Okay," Peter said. He asked, "What now?"

"We've called for backup because we don't know what we're dealing with here, but we've asked them to stand down until we get the women and the cats out."

"Where are you now?" Peter asked.

"Close. Don't worry. We're getting some equipment together. He has the women locked down pretty tight. You folks stay where you are, out of sight there in that thicket. Got it? We'll bring the women and the cats to you."

"Yes, sir. Thank you." After ending the call, Peter said to the others, "They're in a basement room which is locked down pretty tight. They're going to get the women and the cats out, then deal with the scumbag."

"The cats?" Parker asked.

"Yes, they're with the women," Peter said.

"Inside?" Parker asked. "I wondered where they disappeared to. How in the world did they get inside?"

"There's a cat door into that room," Peter explained, "but I guess it isn't where the women can access it to get out. Anyway, the gals and the cats are fine. The police are going to break them out, then go after that kidnapper freak."

Just then Michael stepped in front of Parker and the boys and hissed, "Who's there?"

"That's what I want to know," the man behind the flashlight said. "Who are you, and what are you doing out here? This is private property, you know."

"Shhhh," Michael said, glancing toward the house. "There's a rescue in progress. The police are involved."

“Rescue?” the man repeated. “Police? At the old Stanley place?” He laughed. “Well that’s rich, ’cause there’s no one there. I can tell you no one lives there. I’m caretaker for the old Stanley place, but not for long. It’s doomed to be demolished, like so many other grand old houses.”

“Well, someone’s in there now,” Peter said. “See the car in the driveway?” I believe there’s another car on the property as well—maybe in the garage. Is there a garage?”

The man shook his head. “No, but there’s a big old barn around the other side. Yeah,” he said, “that car you see there belongs to a nephew. He comes around sometimes to check on things. He’s the only family member who’s still on his feet, if you know what I mean. Most are under the ground, and those who are above ground are feeble of mind and limb.” He chuckled. “Either crazy in the head or in a wheelchair or both. So Calvie comes along and he checks in once in a while.” He tapped his own head and said, “He’s a bit touched, if you ask me. What a goofball his parents raised.” He cocked his head. “You say a rescue? Who’s being rescued? What’s that about?”

Ignoring his question, Michael asked, “Have you been inside there lately?”

“On no, I’m not allowed inside, nor do I want to go inside. Those people are kind of paranoid and if something were to go missing…no, my job is to keep people off the property.”

"I doubt you get much traffic out here," Peter said.

The man tilted his head. "An occasional lookie-loo—you know, someone who pulls in to take a look. If I see that going on, I chase them off." He added, "They could be looking for a gang hideaway or a place to do their drugs, you know."

"So the Stanley family owns the place?" Peter asked.

"Yeah, they came here from the east maybe half a century ago. They was kinda crazy, like—you know peculiar, I guess you'd say. One day they left here—all of them. Well, there weren't many, really. As they were leaving, one of the kinfolk came by my place…" he pointed, "…down the lane about a mile. They asked if I'd watch the old house and keep people off the property. They gave me $5,000 to do it. Most of it's still in the bank." He looked in the direction of the Stanley house. "So you say Calvie needs rescuing? What happened to him? And why are you people hiding out here in the grove?" He held out his hand. "By the way, I'm Marsh—it's Marshall, but they call me Marsh." He laughed. "In school I was Marshmallow, as you can imagine." He looked at the boys. "Do kids still give crazy and sometimes hurtful nicknames in school?" Before they could respond, he asked, "Do you have nicknames? What are your names?"

"I'm Simon, and this is Adam. I've been called Simple Simon and Simon Says. Dad had to explain what those names mean." He shook his head. "I'd never heard of either of those things."

Marsh chuckled and looked at Adam. "Are you Adam's Apple?"

"Huh?" Adam asked. He shook his head. "Not really."

Marsh turned his attention back to the men. "So what's the deal at the house there? What's going on?"

At that moment Adam said, "Whoa, did you hear that?"

"What was that?" Marsh asked, looking around. "Sounded like a bomb blast."

"Probably a battering ram," Michael said, moving to where he could see the house through the shrubbery.

"Someone's doing damage to the house?" Marsh shrieked. "They can't be doing that. Not on my watch," he said, running in that direction.

Michael and Peter glanced at each other, then they both took off at a dead run and tackled Marsh, dragging him back into the shelter of the foliage.

"What's wrong with you people?" Marsh shouted. "Let me go! I have to do my job!"

"Listen, buddy," Michael said, holding tightly to the man. He looked into Marsh's face. "Your Calvie, there, has kidnapped our wives, and he's holding them hostage in that big old house. The police are in the process of rescuing them right this minute, so we don't need you messing anything up. Got it?"

"Oh!" Marsh said, relaxing a bit. "Calvie's a kidnapper?"

"At least," Peter said, watching for any sign of movement in the dwindling light of day.

***

Minutes earlier the two police officers had discussed their plan of attack. The sergeant said, "I think I'd rather take the door down than try to get them out through the cat flap. We don't know what we're dealing with as far as that heavy piece of furniture the women described."

"Right," Officer Turner agreed. "Either way, it's going to be noisy, but the house is surrounded, so it doesn't matter now. No matter where he is in there, he won't be able to escape. Once we alert the team that the women are safe, they'll move in on him."

"How about the window?" Sergeant Babcock asked. "What's that thing made of, anyway?"

"I don't know, but the women said there are metal bars—a grate over the window on the inside."

"Okay, the battering ram it is," the sergeant said, lifting it out of the car. "Ready?" he asked moments later, getting in position outside the door.

Officer Turner nodded. "Yeah."

The sergeant looked the situation over and said, "He sure made it impossible for anyone to get in or out of that room, didn't he? Not only does he have these deadbolts, there are padlocks. Okay," he said, "on three."

The sound of the battering ram against the metal door not once or twice, but three times, reverberated through the quiet dusk.

"Are you ladies okay?" Officer Turner asked, pushing the door open.

"Yes," Rochelle said, breathlessly. "Yes, thank you."

"Then follow me," she said. "I have a light. I'll take you to your families."

"Wait," Savannah said. "The cats…where are the cats? They ran when they heard the noise. Did they go outside?"

The officer shined the light into the dark corners of the room and said, "I don't see any cats. They could have taken the cat door out. Come on. Let's get you to safety, then we'll see about the cats."

"Oh, this feels so good," Rochelle said, stepping out into the chill of the evening.

Savannah followed behind, her eyes darting left and right. "Rags," she called quietly. "Olivia."

"Ma'am," the officer whispered, "please. We can't jeopardize the two of you for any cats."

"But you don't understand," Savannah said quietly.

Rochelle took Savannah's arm. "Come on, honey. Rags is okay. You know he always lands on his feet. Let's go now."

"I'm sorry," Savannah said, joining the others. "Yes, let's go."

"Savannah! Rochelle!" Adam called when he saw the women approaching with the police officer.

"Oh, Adam," Savannah said, wrapping her arms around him. "It's wonderful to see you."

"You too," Adam said, hugging her tightly.

He looked around. "Where's Rags? Didn't Rags find you?"

She nodded, tears rolling down her cheeks. "He sure did, and Olivia, but they took off again, maybe out the cat door." She looked around. "They didn't come back here?"

"No," Parker said, stepping forward, "but they're together, right? I'm sure they'll find us. They know we're here."

Savannah fought back tears as she enveloped Parker in a hug. "Thank you, dear friend."

"For what?" Parker asked, embracing Savannah.

She pulled back and said, "For going above and beyond the call of duty and obviously helping my family. I really, really appreciate it." Savannah peered into the darkness and said, "So Rags and Olivia know where you guys are?"

Parker nodded. "They kept pulling against their leashes in that direction, so Adam suggested maybe the cats could lead the police to the portion of the house where you were being held—if, indeed, you were inside there someplace. So they found you?" Parker asked. "They led the police to you?"

"Yes," Rochelle said. She held out her hand. "You're Parker? I'm Rochelle. Thank you so much. Your cat, Olivia, she's such a sweetheart."

Parker smiled and looked out over the property, hoping to see the calico. She asked, "Are you boys watching for the cats?"

"Yeah," Simon said. "That's just about all we've been doing, is trying to watch Rags," the boy complained. "He's—what do you call it—a pocket full."

Rochelle tousled the boy's hair and laughed. "A handful?"

"Yes," he said, grabbing her around the waist. "I sure missed you, Mom."

"And I missed you more than you can imagine," she said, holding him close." Rochelle reached out for Peter, who embraced her and Simon together.

Peter kissed Rochelle's face and smoothed her hair. "I was so worried," he said, his voice cracking. When he stepped back, Simon slipped out from between them, and Peter asked, "Did he…? I mean…"

"No," Rochelle said. "No. It was horrifying, but no he didn't touch us."

"Oh, hon," Michael said, when Savannah fell into his arms, "I prayed for this moment. I'm so thankful."

"Me, too," she said, clinging to him.

After several moments Michael pulled away. "Your mom," he said.

Savannah looked around. "Is she here? The children…"

"No, they're at home. I need to call her."

"Where's Blossom?" Rochelle asked.

"She's at home," Simon said. "The cats came home today."

"So you lost track of Rags?" Michael asked before he called his mother-in-law.

Savannah nodded ruefully. "Yes, and Olivia. I'm so worried, Michael. After they got the door open with that big piece of metal, we couldn't find them. The officers wouldn't let us look for them." She grimaced. "They just have to be okay. Who knows what that man might do?"

"What makes you think he'll even see them, or that he'd pay any attention to them? Michael asked.

"Oh, Michael, you know better than that. Rags is probably on the prowl for that crazy kidnapper."

Rather than respond, Michael handed Savannah his phone. "It's your mom. She needs to hear your voice."

"Of course," Savannah said, taking the phone. "Hi, Mom. I'm okay, just exhausted. I'll see you tomorrow. Hug the kids for me. I miss them so much."

"I know, honey. I'm just thankful that you're safe. Get your rest and we'll see you tomorrow."

"I love you, Mom," Savannah said. "Thank you for being there for us." She ended the call and handed the phone back to Michael. When she saw Parker staring into the darkness, she clutched her friend's arm and said, "I'm so sorry. I should have…" She frowned. "Why did you let her go? Was that Rags's doing?"

Parker shook her head. "No. Olivia insisted. She wasn't about to be left behind." When Parker saw tears forming in Savannah's eyes again, she said, "It will be okay. Like I said, the cats know where we are."

"Well, I guess if you're not worried, I shouldn't be," Savannah said unconvincingly. "But it's getting so dark so fast." She glanced around and added, "I suppose they'll see the glow coming from the dome light in the car. That should be just enough to light their way."

"Cats can see in the dark," Simon reminded her.

Savannah smiled at him, but before she could respond, she saw a stranger standing off to the side looking at them. "Michael," she whispered, "who's that?"

"That's Marsh," Michael said. "He's caretaker for the place."

"Really?" Savannah grumped. "Well, where was he when that madman was holding us hostage?"

"He's only responsible for what goes on outside, not inside the house," Michael explained.

"I'm sorry to hear what happened to you ladies, ma'am," Marsh said. "The Stanleys are not going to like this. Not one bit. And I'm not going to be the one to tell them. They may want me to give back some of the money."

Savannah gazed at him for a moment, then focused on the house, which was now lit up from the outside with spotlights.

"Come out with your hands up!" someone bellowed through a bullhorn. "Now!"

Adam and Simon covered their ears with their hands.

Just then Sergeant Babcock trotted up to the onlookers. "I suggest you folks leave. We appreciate your help. The women are safe. Best that you stay that way and go on home."

"But our cats…" Savannah asserted.

Parker moved closer.

"Oh yes," he said, "the cats. Now you're talking about the big grey one and the fluffy colorful one, right?" When Savannah and Parker nodded he said, "They led us to the creep. The cats knew right where he was hiding, and the bigger cat—the grey one—sure acted like he wanted a piece of the dirtbag." He chuckled. "When we saw the cats in the house taking the staircase ahead of us, we didn't pay much attention until they began to act up."

"Act up?" Parker asked.

"Well, they stopped at the top of the stairs and looked back at us. Then they started turning in circles and stuff. Finally, one of our team, a gal who evidently knows cats, motioned for us to follow them. They led us to a closed door, sat down in front of it, and just stared back at us like they were waiting for us to do something."

"So you arrested him?" Savannah asked.

The sergeant shook his head. "No. We confirmed he's inside there, and he's babbling about having a bomb."

"Gads," Savannah said.

"Yeah, one of the S.W.A.T team is trying to talk him down. We have the bomb squad on the way."

"So you don't need the cats anymore," Savannah said.

"Ma'am?" the sergeant questioned.

"You know where he is, now," Savannah said. "You must have someone bring out the cats."

When the sergeant looked down at his feet, she explained, “They’re quite specialized cats, you know. They both work with law enforcement.”

“Is that right?” he asked, looking at the three women. He then pointed. “Parker,” he said. “Parker Campbell? Is that Olivia in there?”

Parker nodded. “And Rags, who works with…”

“Detective Craig Sledge up north,” the sergeant said more enthusiastically. “Yes ma’am.

I’m on it,” he said, walking briskly toward the house.

The onlookers continued to mill around in the thicket together, keeping an eye in the direction of the house through the thick foliage, when they saw the sergeant trotting back toward them.

“Okay,” he said, “we’ve got a problem and we’re going to need your help.”

“What?” Michael asked defensively.

Peter stood alongside Michael.

“He’s threatening to blow up the place.”

“If he thinks we’re still inside,” Rochelle said, “he’s probably serious about doing it. He has threatened us, and I get the impression that he doesn’t care much whether he lives or dies. Yeah, I’d take him seriously.”

“How well do you know him?” the sergeant asked.

"I went all through school with him. We grew up in the same neighborhood, but ran in different circles."

"So you're his target? It was a targeted abduction, wasn't it?" the sergeant asked.

Rochelle nodded. "Yes. He seems to blame me for the way his life turned out. He's a disturbed and unhappy man, and he has things twisted in his mind. He wants revenge. He seems to think that by punishing me, he'll feel better. I tried to talk to him a little about the reality of the situation, but he's obviously on a crazy course designed to hurt himself and anyone who gets in his way."

The officer gazed at Rochelle for a moment, then asked, "Are you a psychologist?"

"I have some training," she said, "but I'm more a psychic than a psycho." She chuckled. "That didn't come out right, did it?"

The others chuckled as well.

The sergeant turned away and spoke into his radio, then returned and said to Rochelle, "Ma'am, I know you've been through a lot, but we need your help."

Before she could speak, Peter walked forward. "No," he said. "She's coming home with me. She's been through enough."

Rochelle patted her husband's chest and asked the officer. "What is it? What do you need help with?"

"I just got word that he's holding one of our officers hostage. Do you think you could talk to Stanley?" The guy keeps calling for Rochelle. 'Just let me talk to Rochelle.'"

"No," Peter said. "I don't want her anywhere near that son of a …. No, Rochelle."

"I agree, sir," the sergeant said. "I don't want to put her in danger either. I'd like to see if he'll listen to her on the phone."

Rochelle let out a long sigh. "Well, I'm exhausted, as you can imagine, but I sure don't want to see anyone get hurt." She looked at Savannah and Parker. "And I will do anything to make sure the cats are spared. Yes, I'll speak with him."

"Excuse me," Savannah said, moving closer to the officer. "Do you know where the cats are now?"

He glanced around. "I just asked and was told they were seen coming out of the house. They could be on their way back here."

"Or that could have been some of the other cats," Savannah said. "There are several other cats on the property." She looked at the house. "You say he has explosives in there?"

The sergeant hesitated, then said, "Possibly."

When the sergeant started to walk away to set up the call between Calvin and Rochelle, Savannah said, "Wait, you said an officer is being held hostage? That's probably where Rags is."

"Why would you say that?" he asked. "Why would a cat be drawn to something like that?"

"I don't know why," Savannah said, "I just know my cat. That's the way he rolls. I guess he thinks he's Robin Hood or something."

"Robin Hood," Simon repeated, chuckling.

"It's not funny," Adam insisted. "You heard the policeman. That guy has a bomb in there."

"Allegedly," the sergeant said, backtracking. "He could be bluffing." He asked, "Did either of you ladies see him with a weapon?"

"Just a gnarly knife," Rochelle said, shuddering.

"Okay, Mrs. Whitcomb, I'll give the word that you will speak with him." Sergeant Babcock walked away with his phone up to his ear, then returned and reported, "We have the two cats." He chuckled. "Officer Rosalind Turner said that as they were retreating to give the jerk the space he negotiated for, the cats ran past them up the stairs. She and Officer Danielle Sparks went after them and they led her to a door where they began scratching. She said the big cat was carrying on something fierce. She was afraid he'd blow their cover, so she tried to retrieve the cats, just as the door opens. The officer backs up against the wall and was surprised to see the hostage walk out before the door slams shut again. Officer Turner and the hostage each grabbed a cat and ran."

"Oh, what a relief," Parker said.

The sergeant chuckled. "According to the hostage, things were getting pretty intense in that room until the cat rattled Mr. Stanley by making all that noise outside the door. It caused him to lose his focus. It appears that he couldn't handle having a hostage while trying to work his plan. So we're back at the drawing board. Now that our officer's not in the way, we can execute a more aggressive takeover." He shook his head. "Those are *some* cats you have there."

"That's Rags and Olivia," Adam boasted

"Yeah," Simon added. "Rags is a police cat."

Sergeant Babcock gazed at the boys, then said, "Well, they can join our force any time they want. The grey one—the bigger one—he doesn't follow orders very well, but he seems to have instincts that could come in handy in a lot of our cases." He suddenly became alert and listened for a moment. "Who's that coming in?" he asked. When the vehicle came closer he groaned. "Wouldn't you know it, it's the media. You gals might want to get out of here while you can. Go home."

"You don't want to interrogate us?" Savannah asked.

"Not tonight. Get your rest. You've been through enough these last thirty-six hours. Come down to the station tomorrow morning and we'll take your statement then." He looked behind them. "Go, before the vultures catch up with you."

"We need to get our cats," Savannah said. "We're not leaving without the cats."

"Oh yeah," he said. "They should be showing up any minute now. Officers Turner and Sparks are bringing them out here."

"So you don't need me to speak with Calvin Stanley?" Rochelle asked.

"No," the sergeant said. "I don't want to involve you unless it's absolutely imperative." He started to walk off toward the house when a woman ran up to the onlookers with a microphone. A man followed with lights and a camera.

"What happened here?" the woman asked. "Is it a hostage situation?"

When no one spoke, Simon volunteered, "My mom and Savannah were kidnapped and our cats found them,"

"Simon," Peter warned.

"Yeah, one of the cats is Rags," Adam said. "He's famous. He's in books and he works for the police in Hammond. He saved Savannah and Rochelle and a policeman."

The sergeant winced. "Well, so much for keeping a cap on it, right?" He said to the reporter, "Okay, I'll make one statement, then let these people go home, okay?" He did a head count. "You're not all going to fit into that car." He asked, "Who's car is this?"

Peter raised his hand.

"Well, you take the two victims and maybe the boys; we'll have someone shuttle the rest of you back home. Come on, ladies," he said, holding a car door open for Savannah and Rochelle.

Savannah held back. "Not without the cats."

"There he is!" Adam shouted. "There's Rags. See him?"

"Oh, thank goodness!" Savannah exclaimed, taking Rags from an officer. She asked, "Adam, do you have his leash?"

"Yes," he said, running to the car and retrieving it. He snapped it onto Rags's harness as Savannah held him. She ran her hand over Olivia after Parker took the cat from another officer. "I am so happy to see you both," she said, watching Parker fasten Olivia's leash to her harness.

"You two are grounded for the rest of the night," Parker said, kissing the top of Olivia's head. "What do you think you were you doing, anyway?" she asked.

Officer Turner chuckled. "They were working with us."

"Mostly getting in the way, I imagine," Savannah said.

"No ma'am," the officer said.

"Were they really heroes?" Simon asked, eagerly?

"Yeah, they found the hostage," Adam said.

"They did more than that," Officer Turner said.

Both boys said, "Really?"

She smiled at them. "Well, they ran right into our staging area. We were just getting in position to approach the house. A couple of us tried to catch them. I wanted to get them back to you, but they were wily. It got a little hairy there for a minute. We could tell there was something different about those two. One of our team—a gal who has a lot of cats—decided they were trying to get us to follow them, so she did. They led her to an outbuilding. There was a car in there. Your car?" she asked.

"Probably mine," Rochelle said.

"Officer Sparks called me to help. The keys were in it. When we saw what else was in there, we got that taken care of, then we loaded the cats into the car and drove it away from the house."

"What was in there?" Savannah asked.

When the sergeant saw the cameraman continuing to film, he walked forward and asked them to return to their van. "This is an active situation, we need you to back off. Leave the victims alone. Just get back. It'll all be over soon if everyone cooperates."

Rochelle watched as the cameraman and reporter walked away, then she asked, quietly, "Explosives?" When the others looked at her, she shrugged and said, "I think my senses are coming back. I sense explosives."

The officer nodded. "Yes, all hidden carefully in your car. The bomb squad had arrived by the time the cats showed us where your car was parked. There was no detonator, but a lighted match or a spark sure would have sent that car through the roof."

Officer Sparks said, "I've known a lot of cats, but I've never known one to sniff out explosives."

"What else did they do?" Adam asked. "I mean the cats."

"Yeah," Michael said, "how did they get back into the house where the officer was being held?"

Officer Turner glanced at her partner and said, "Wily—those two are wily. You give them an inch and they take a mile. They managed to get away from us, and they ran past everyone and went back into the house. After that fiasco calmed down, we got a good grip on the cats and managed to deliver them back to you."

"Yes," Officer Sparks said, "we sure didn't want to leave them inside. He keeps threatening that he has explosives in the room with him. We just wanted to take the cats a safe distance away from there."

"Thank you so much," Savannah gushed.

"Yes," Parker said, snuggling with Olivia. "Thank you."

"You're welcome," Officer Turner said. Just as the two officers turned to leave, the night sky lit up. There was a deafening blast, and debris began to fall all around them.

Savannah held tightly to Rags, and Michael instinctively tried to shelter her.

"He did it," Rochelle muttered, shrinking into Peter's embrace. Simon buried his face in her jacket sleeve. "He blew up the whole house."

***

"Is everyone all right?" Officer Turner asked, sounding a little breathless.

"I think so," Rochelle said, holding Simon and looking around at the others.

"Adam?" Michael called, his arms around Savannah and Rags.

"He's here with me," Parker said from under the bows of a large tree. "We're okay."

The officer gazed at the burning house and murmured, "I guess there may not be an arrest made tonight, after all."

Chapter Seven

Late that night after everyone had gone to bed at the Whitcombs', including Parker, who accepted an invitation to stay there with Olivia rather than make the drive back to her condo, Savannah had awakened. "Michael," she hissed. "Michael, wake up."

"What?" he grumbled. He rubbed his eyes and pushed up on one elbow. "What are you doing up, hon?"

"I can't find Rags," she said.

"Oh, Savannah," he moaned. "He's probably in the kitchen eating kibbles or sleeping with Simon's cats."

"No, he's not," she said. "I went to get a drink of water, and I don't see him anywhere. Michael, something's wrong."

"What makes you say that?"

"Well, he usually stays close to me after something like what happened this week. You know, he becomes my therapy cat," she explained.

He winced. "I have to agree. I've seen him become Velcro on you after you've been hurt or something." He sat up. "Did you look under the bed? In the closet?"

She nodded. "Yes, I have. Michael I don't think he's in the house. Would you go outside with me?" She pulled her robe around her lithe frame. "I'm a little afraid to go out alone after…"

"You think he got out, but how, Savannah?"

"I don't know how," she spat. "All I know is he's not in the house. Come on, Michael."

"Okay, let's go," he said, putting on a jacket over his pajamas and slipping into his shoes. He walked with her through the living room and toward the front door.

"Savannah!" Rochelle exclaimed, greeting the couple from the kitchen. "Can't you guys sleep? Me neither. I wanted to get a couple of pain relievers."

"Oh, Rochelle!" Savannah yelped, startled. "Are you all right?"

"Just a little achy, is all," she said. "That was a lot of stress, and my muscles took a hit."

"I know what you mean," Savannah said.

"So are *you* feeling okay?" Rochelle asked. "Do you need anything?"

"I'm okay. It's just that we can't find Rags." Savannah asked, "He's not in *your* room, is he?"

"I don't think so," Rochelle said, "but he might be in the room with the boys."

"I checked." Michael said. He asked, "Hey, did you hear anything else from the sergeant after we went to bed? Did they find that scumbag in the rubble?"

Rochelle shook her head. "No. We didn't hear from anyone. I guess that means their search was inconclusive or they're still searching."

"Oh, they probably didn't want to bother us late at night," Savannah suggested.

"Peter told them to call us any time," Rochelle said. "He kept his phone next to the bed. He's eager to know that Calvin Stanley is either in custody or dead."

"There you are," Peter said, joining the others.

"Sorry if we woke you," Savannah said. When Olivia walked into the room and stretched her front paws out in front of her, her fluffy tail arching over her back, Savannah cooed, "Hi there, sweet Olivia. Did we wake you, too? I'm sorry." She walked toward the sunroom and whispered, "I'll close the door so we don't bother your mommy."

"Too late," Parker called from inside the room. "What's all the commotion?" she asked, stepping into the living room with the others and buttoning the robe Rochelle had loaned her. "What's going on?"

Peter yawned. "Yeah, what's everyone doing up, for heaven's sake?"

"Rags is missing again," Rochelle reported.

"Oh no," Parker said. "What's he up to now?"

"I wonder…" Peter started.

"What, Peter?" Savannah asked. "Do you know where he is?"

He winced. "Well, I might have maybe let him out earlier. I thought I heard something, and I came out to look around. When I didn't see anything, I opened the front door. I thought I felt something slip past me, but saw nothing, so I came on back inside and went to bed. Do you think Rags might have…?"

"Yeah," Michael groaned, "taken advantage of you. But why?" he asked, looking at Savannah.

"Who knows?" she said, opening the front door. "Rags!" she called. "Rags, kitty-kitty."

"There he is," Rochelle said. "Is that him?"

Savannah and Michael looked in the direction Rochelle pointed. "That's him," Savannah said. "You come back here, you little…" When he walked up to her, Savannah stooped to pick him up, but he skittered a few feet away, stopped, and looked back at her. She walked toward him again, and again he ran a short distance away and stopped. When he turned in place and meowed, she said, "He wants to show me something." She looked pleadingly at Michael. "Come on, I'm not going anywhere alone tonight. Let's see what he wants."

"Oh, Savannah," Michael complained, "don't you think you need your sleep more than he needs to be pacified?"

She faced him. "You think he's just playing games? Well, I don't think so. He wants to show us something, and I want to see what it is. Come on."

"What is it, Rags?" Michael asked, trudging with the others along the lighted pathway. When the cat stopped and looked at Michael's veterinary truck, Michael asked, "You want to go for a ride?" He chuckled guardedly. "Maybe he wants to go home. He probably misses the children and Peaches."

Just then Simon called from the front door, "Daaad!"

"We're right here, Son," Peter said. "There's nothing for you to worry about. You go back to sleep, now."

"But Dad, it's your phone. The police department called your phone. It kept ringing so I got up. Here, I got it for you. You'd better call them back."

"Oh, I'm sorry," Peter said. "I didn't mean for it to wake you." He walked briskly toward Simon and took his phone. "Thanks, Son," he said, walking a distance away to check his missed calls.

"What are you guys doing out here?" Simon asked.

"Looking for Rags," Michael said. "He seems to want to go for a ride or something." He walked closer to his truck and reached for the door handle.

"No!" Peter shouted. "Don't touch it!"

"What?" Michael asked, taking a couple of steps back.

"Oh my gosh," Peter said. He took a breath and blew it out. "That was close."

"What are you talking about?" Michael asked.

"Where are you going, Savannah?" Peter asked.

"To get Rags. He keeps acting like he wants to go for a ride in Michael's truck."

"Okay," Peter said. "Get the cat, but don't touch anything. Simon, you stay here, I'll go get Adam. Michael, help me get our cats, would you?" He looked at Parker, who held Olivia in her arms, and said. "Good, you've got her. Stay out here and don't touch anything." He then said, "Oh no, the birds." He handed Simon his flashlight and said, "Son, go around to the backyard and free the birds."

"What?" Simon cried. "Let them go? Dad, what's wrong?"

"Do as I say, and hurry!" Peter shouted. Before stepping back inside with Michael, he said, "A police van is coming to get us. We could be in danger here, and so could the animals. Hurry, now. Come on."

"Okay, what's going on?" Michael asked scant minutes later as Peter led the group along their front path, away from the house.

"There's the van," Peter said. "Let's go."

"But Clayton and Matilda," Simon wailed. "They'll get lost. Why did you make me let them out of the cage?"

"I'm sorry, Son," Peter said, nudging the boy forward into the van. "Let's get inside, quickly, now, and I'll tell you what's happened." Once he heard the door slide shut, Peter leaned back against his seat with Minnie in his arms and spoke deliberately and quietly, "Calvin Stanley is thought to have survived the blast, and the police have reason to believe that he found his way over here and that he may have set at least one explosive somewhere on our property. A team is on their way. The whole area will be evacuated."

"Good Lord," Michael muttered. He sat forward and glanced around outside. "There they are," he said. "Gads, look at all the squad cars."

"Those officers are on evacuation detail," the driver said. "The bomb squad won't be far behind." He chuckled. "They're busy tonight."

"There have been other reports of bombs?" Savannah asked.

"Just two—the one out at the Stanley place and this one," the driver said.

Rochelle and Savannah gasped.

Everyone sat with their own thoughts for a few minutes, then Savannah said, "Michael's truck."

"What?" Peter asked.

"Peter, tell the police that the bomb is probably in or around Michael's truck. That's what Rags was trying to tell us. I'm sure of it," Savannah said. "Oh my gosh, he must have heard or sensed someone outside there. Maybe he saw that creep monkeying with the truck. Peter, tell the bomb squad to check the veterinary truck in your driveway."

"I can make the call," the driver said. "But now you want me to tell them that a cat has sniffed out explosives in a veterinary truck. Is that what you said?"

"Yes," Savannah asserted.

He glanced curiously at her in the rearview mirror and said, "Okay. If you say so." When he ended the call he asked, "Where do you folks want to go? Do you know someone you could stay with until this mess is cleared up?"

"You could all come to my condo," Parker suggested. "It's small, but we could make do."

"That's nice of you, Parker," Peter said, "but the sergeant I spoke with suggested an alternative." He addressed their driver. "He said you have safe place at the station for people in situations like this."

The driver nodded. "Yes, it's ready and waiting if that's what you want to do."

In tears, Rochelle said, "But for how long? We can't stay there forever, and I can tell you that we'll never be safe until that man is in custody or dead. He'll keep trying to hurt me and anyone around me."

The driver glanced at her. "As I understand it this was a targeted abduction. Mr. Stanley had something against one of you." He asked, "Was that you?"

"Yes," Rochelle said, weakly.

"What do you know about Mr. Stanley?" he asked. "Is there something you could tell us that might give us a clue about what we could do next? What are his interests?"

"Making my life miserable," Rochelle said. She sat up straighter and said, "Yes, if he knew where I was going to be he might try to come there. Is there any way you could use a decoy and put it on the radio or internet where that person—you know, someone impersonating me—where she'll be?"

"Great idea," Parker said. "Let me do it."

Savannah frowned. "Oh, I'm sure they could use a policewoman." She turned in her seat. "Do you suppose he's watching us now?"

"I doubt it," the driver said. "He wouldn't stick around if he expected an explosion." He nodded. "Hey, there go the bomb squad to your place now."

"Gosh, I hope they get there in time," Rochelle said, her voice pinched.

"I hope Clayton and Matilda are safe," Simon said. He asked, "Will they come back, Dad? Will Clayton and Matilda come back?"

Peter winced. "I sure hope so, Son. I think they're happy with us and they know where their food comes from. I'm sure they will." More quietly, he said, "I just hope they don't hang around too close, in case…"

Minutes later their driver pulled the van up in front of the police station. The occupants were quickly ushered inside and led to a large room with futons scattered around one area and a table with coffee and snacks in a corner. There were magazines, a TV, and even a phone-charging and wifi station.

"Wow! It looks like they were expecting overnight guests," Michael said.

"Yes, we sometimes get them," the driver said. "This is a brainchild of our captain's wife—to maintain a safe room for people in need, whether it's a homeless family, someone misplaced after a house fire, or…last week we hosted a young family. They were traveling through when they were robbed. It's not the Ritz, but it's awfully nice to have a place to crash when you really need it."

"It sure is," Peter said. "Thank you."

"Thank the local women's club. They keep it maintained and all. We just provide the space." He pointed. "There's a bathroom just down the hall there. Please, make yourselves and the cats at home. Oh, there's a litter box in the closet with a fresh supply of litter, I believe. Let me get it for you."

Michael joined him to offer his help and said, "My gosh, you even have cat food in here."

"The ladies think of everything." The driver chuckled. "We housed a couple of horses once. We have an equine unit with corrals out back, and we hosted visiting horses that night when the gals—two gals heading for a rodeo—broke down and needed a safe place to stay."

Savannah grinned. "I guess you can't get much safer than a police station."

"Do you think he knows where I am?" Rochelle asked a while later, holding a cup of tea in her hands.

"I think he probably does," Parker said. She put a hand on Rochelle, "I like the idea of the decoy. Someone to lead him away from you, Rochelle, and into a trap." She shook her head. "Man, he's cunning, isn't he?"

"Seems to be," Rochelle agreed.

Savannah thought for a moment, then said, "But he doesn't seem to do well when things don't go his way. He's meticulous in his planning, but when his plan is interrupted he gets a little rattled. Did you notice that, Rochelle?"

"Yes," she said. "Yes, you're right. So he's bound to get sloppy. To make mistakes. It appears that his obsession is at an all-time high, but yes, he definitely seems to be getting more careless."

Just then they heard a soft knock at the door. It opened and a man asked, "May I come in?"

"Certainly," Peter said, "it's your station," he joked.

The officer smiled. "I'm Dr. Darrel Gray. I coordinate some of the more hazardous incidents—when we're dealing with someone who believes he has nothing to lose and who may be dangerously obsessed with harming others, for example. There's often a psychological aspect to situations like these, and I often work here as a psychology consultant." He glanced around at everyone. "I'm sure sorry to hear what you've been through this week. Who are the victims?"

"All of us," Michael said. "We were all victimized by that lowlife jerk." He motioned toward Savannah and Rochelle. "But my wife and her friend were held hostage."

"Two of you? Were you both a target?" he asked.

"Just me," Rochelle said quietly.

Dr. Gray winced. "I'm awfully sorry. It's a horrible thing when someone takes away your freedom and worse when he puts your life and the life of your loved ones at risk." He tilted his head. "I hear there were cats involved. Some very brave cats."

"Rags and Olivia," Simon said. "And Blossom."

"Which one is that that you're petting?" the doctor asked.

"This is Blossom," Simon said. "That man took Blossom and Rags, too, but he turned them loose and they had to find their way back home all by themselves."

"Yeah, and they got really sore paws from all that walking to get back home," Adam added.

Dr. Gray cocked his head. "The cats found their way home? How far did they have to walk?"

Adam looked at his dad. "About eight miles?" he questioned.

Michael nodded.

"This is Rags," Adam said, running his hand over the cat's fur as he lay next to Adam on a futon. The boy pointed. "That's Olivia. Rags and Olivia helped the police last night."

"Yeah," Simon said energetically, "they found Mom and Savannah and the bad guy. They showed the police where the bad guy was hiding."

"I heard about that," Dr. Gray said, "and I have to tell you, that's a first. I've never…" he stopped and squinted down at Rags. "Did you say that cat's name is Rags?" He glanced around the room. "You people aren't from Hammond, are you? Do you know Detective Sledge?"

Savannah smiled. "Yes. Rags works with the detective sometimes."

"Indeed he does," Dr. Gray said. "Well, I'll be. I'll have to get a picture with him before you leave. This is quite an honor." He glanced around the room and quipped, "There are cats everywhere.

I don't think we've ever run a cat shelter in here." He cleared his throat and spoke with more authority, "I hear that one of you volunteered to be a decoy to try to trap the perp."

Everyone looked at Parker and she nodded. "I'm willing to do that. Rochelle and I are about the same size and have the same coloring…"

"And your name is…"

"Parker," she said, "Parker Campbell."

He sat back and said, "And Olivia. Oh, yes. I know your reputation, Ms. Campbell. You're obviously not new to police work."

"Well, I haven't been through the academy or anything," she admitted.

He gazed at her for a moment, then asked Rochelle, "So what do you know about the perp? I've been briefed, but maybe you can tell me more. We know that he has some sort of obsession with you."

"He blames me for his awful life—missing out on experiencing a prom…"

"High school prom?" He asked. "His pain goes back that far?"

Rochelle nodded. "His parents were strict in an odd way. Calvin had no childhood—well, not like most children experience. He was inside studying all the time. He had no experience in learning social skills and he didn't know how to make friends. It seems that he blames me because he wasn't included in my social circle. He might have had a crush on me and he has decided to put the blame for his unhappy life on me." Rochelle continued, "I was nice to him. I often invited him to join us, but his mother wouldn't allow him out of the house. I felt sorry seeing him always looking out his bedroom window watching the rest of us play."

"So he liked you. You were kind to him. You made him feel less lonely, but he also hated you or, as you said, blamed you, for not doing more—for letting him down in some way."

"I guess so," Rochelle said. She began to cry. "I had no idea that a kindness could backfire into something like this. It's just not fair."

"No, it's not, but remember, Mrs. Whitcomb, we're not dealing with a logical person. And you did not create his state of mind."

She looked up. "Thank you for saying that. Sometimes when something like this happens, you get the urge to withdraw from all of humanity. Thank you for reminding me that this nightmare is an isolated situation."

"Yes, in a way," Dr. Gray said. "People are targeted for various reasons all day and night. It's human nature, at least for some, to place blame. Friendships are dissolved because of blame—marriages, business partnerships—all sorts of relationships, and too often that blame is misguided because of a warped belief system—a warped sense of reality." He looked at Parker. "I think your idea might work in this case. We don't know where he is or what he has up his sleeve, but we're pretty sure he knows where Rochelle is—that she's here. It's likely that he watched you folks leave your house in the van."

"You think he could be here?" Peter shouted angrily. "Out there somewhere waiting for Rochelle?"

"Our officers are aware of that possibility, and they're detaining anyone they see loitering in the area. But he could be inside one of the buildings around us, on the street with the homeless…"

"I gave one of the officers a description," Rochelle said.

"Yes, we have it from both you and Mrs. Ivey, but keep in mind that he could change his appearance and probably has."

"Sir," Simon said.

"Don't interrupt, Son," Peter scolded.

"But, Dad," the boy said.

Peter held up his hand to stop him.

"Let him speak," the doctor said. "He could be part of the solution."

"Yeah," Simon said, "Adam and I saw a beard in his car."

"You saw his car?" the doctor asked, surprised. "When was that? This morning?"

"No, yesterday," Simon said. "We saw it at the park where he took Mom and Savannah. We went there to look for clues and we saw a car parked all crazy. Adam and I looked inside, and we saw a black beard and bandanas, rope, and…"

"We saw that car at the old house that blew up, too," Adam said.

"A black beard, huh?" Dr. Gray said. He took out a pad and pen. "What else did you boys see in there?"

After listening to what the boys had to say, the doctor asked, "Did anyone get a plate number?" When no one answered, he asked, "What's the make and year?"

"An older black sedan, maybe a Honda or Toyota," Michael said. He looked at Peter, who nodded.

"Wasn't the car demolished in the blast?" Peter asked.

The doctor shrugged. "We'll have to find out."

"That should help you catch him, right?" Simon asked.

"Yeah, but it's easy for people to change their appearance, their vehicle…criminals use all kinds of tricks." When he saw the mood in the room take a dive, he added, "But we always get our man…or woman." The doctor stood up and motioned toward Rochelle and Parker. "Okay, I want you two to exchange clothes and…" Before he could continue there was another knock at the door.

He opened it, then excused himself and left the room.

Dr. Gray returned with Sergeant Babcock, "Good morning," he greeted. He looked down at his watch and continued, "Yes, it is morning—almost sunup."

The sergeant cleared his throat and announced, "They found explosives at the Whitcomb house." He looked at the cats. "Did I hear that a cat led our officers to the explosives?"

"In my truck?" Michael asked.

"Yes, that's where they found them. They're using bomb-sniffing dogs inside the house now and around the property." He chuckled. "They had a little trouble getting the dogs to focus at the back of the house because they were being dive-bombed by a couple of birds." He looked at Peter and Rochelle. "Do you have a bird problem around there?"

This caught Simon's attention. "Birds?"

"Yes, parrots, from what I'm told," the sergeant said.

Simon blurted, "Clayton and Matilda! They're still at home."

Rochelle and Peter smiled at the boy.

"So they are your birds?" The sergeant asked. "Did you know the birds aren't in their cage? I understand there's a large cage on your property."

Peter nodded. "We turned them loose so they could get away in case…" he choked up.

The sergeant gazed at the cats, asking, "Which one found the explosives?"

Adam ran his hand over Rags. "This one."

"Is that your cat?" he asked.

Adam nodded, then motioned toward Michael and Savannah. "Well, our cat."

Sergeant Babcock addressed the Iveys. "We might need his help again. What would you say to…?"

Michael said, "Sure, I'll take him over there…"

"Or our dog handler can…" Sergeant Babcock started.

Savannah shook her head. "Oh no. That wouldn't work."

The sergeant tilted his head. "Why not?"

"Cats and dogs work completely differently," Savannah explained. "Please let Michael go with you."

"Good," the sergeant muttered. "Okay, then what I'd like to do, once the house is cleared, is take you, Ms. Campbell, to the Whitcomb home on the ploy that you are Mrs. Whitcomb. We're taking you there on the ruse that you're going to pick up a few things, then rejoin your family in a hotel until the home is cleared for you to return. We'll leave you there and give him the opportunity to show himself."

"But," Savannah said, obviously concerned.

"No worries, Mrs. Ivey," he said. "There will be officers inside the house. Even if he is at the house, watching—which I doubt—he probably isn't calculating enough—clear-headed enough, at this point—to notice how many officers went in and how many are coming out. In fact, I doubt he's even on that site. He's probably here someplace, watching." He faced Parker. "Once you're inside, an officer will usher you to a safe place and wait for Mr. Stanley to make his move."

"And do you still want Rags over there?" Michael asked.

"Yes," the sergeant said. "If you and the cat will come with me…" He gazed at Parker. "You be ready when I return with Mr. Ivey and the cat. We want to make sure the dogs didn't miss anything."

"Okay," Parker said. She grinned at Rochelle and quipped. "Want to change pajamas?"

"Yeah, we *are* still in our PJs, aren't we?" Rochelle said. "What time is it?"

Michael looked at his watch. "Almost six."

"It's morning time?" Adam asked.

"Yes," the sergeant said, squeezing the boy's shoulder. He smiled. "I'm told that donuts will be arriving just about any time."

Adam and Simon grinned eagerly at one another.

***

"So there are no more explosives?" Peter asked when Michael and the sergeant returned to the safe room nearly an hour later with Rags. "The cat didn't find anything the dogs missed?"

"No more explosives," Michael said. He patted Simon's arm, just as the boy started to take a bite of a jelly donut, and said, "And Clayton and Matilda are safe in their pen."

"Really?" Simon asked. "Cool."

Michael nodded. "They were already inside; I just latched the door."

"Thanks, Mr. Michael," Simon said, biting into the donut.

"But what if he brings another bomb to the house?" Rochelle asked, concerned.

The sergeant sat down next to her and spoke softly. "There are three officers inside your home and four hidden outside—one on each side of the property. Mr. Stanley won't be dropping off anything or taking anything from your property and getting away with it." He looked Rochelle in the eye. "Your nightmare is almost over, Mrs. Whitcomb. We'll get him, then you can go home and return to your peaceful life."

"Thank you," she managed, her eyes welling up with tears.

"Ready, Ms. Campbell?" Sergeant Gray asked. He noticed, "Good, there's a hood on that coat Mrs. Whitcomb was wearing. Keep it on. We don't want anyone getting a close look at you."

"Got it," Parker said, standing up with Olivia in her arms.

He stopped her. “Um…maybe we’d better leave the cat here.”

“I’d rather take her with me,” she countered. “She can be helpful in a situation like this.”

He glanced at Rochelle. “But will he know that’s not Mrs. Whitcomb’s cat? We don’t want a tiny detail like that blowing our plans all to hell.”

Rochelle shook her head. “I don’t think he’ll give it a second thought or even notice.”

“I agree,” Savannah said. “From what I got, he’s beyond focusing on details like that. His obsession with hurting Rochelle is too all-consuming.” She glanced at Parker. “I agree with her that Olivia could be useful. She’s super-intuitive and has probably been down a road similar to this before.”

Parker nodded.

“Okay then, but do me a favor. Can you carry her more hidden, like under the coat?” the sergeant asked.

“Sure,” Parker said, tucking Olivia inside Rochelle’s coat with her.

The officer ushered Parker out of the room, stopping at the reception desk. He announced rather loudly, “I’m taking Mrs. Whitcomb back to her house now.” While Parker stood a distance away, the hood concealing her identity, he continued, “She’s going to put a few things together that her family might need over the next few days. I’ll go back and pick her up when she’s ready.”

"Cool," the receptionist said. "Good bye, Mrs. Whitcomb."

Parker nodded from under the hood.

The officer drove into the Whitcombs' driveway, climbed out of the car, then opened the passenger door. When Parker stepped out and walked toward the front door, he called, "Have a good day, Mrs. Whitcomb," and he drove away.

Parker let herself into the house with a key Peter had given her, and she noticed that the blinds and drapes were closed. She glanced around the room, feeling a sense of relief when a uniformed female officer approached from the kitchen. "Ms. Campbell?" she asked.

Parker nodded and squatted to allow Olivia to jump down onto the floor. She held tightly to the leash and looked around. "Are you the only officer here?" she asked. "I thought…"

The officer smiled. "I'm Officer Blaire Olivares; you can call me Blaire. No I'm not alone here, there are four officers placed strategically around the property outside and two others watching from inside here. Come on, let me show you to your safe place," she said, ushering Parker into an interior room the Whitcombs obviously used as an office.

Thank you," Parker said. She watched the officer walk out of the room and close the door behind her. She looked around and thought, *At least I can read if I want to. Rochelle and Peter have a nice library.* She quickly chose a mystery and sat down to read. She was just getting into the story when Olivia jumped up into the leather chair with her. "Oh," she yelped. "No scratching on this chair, Olivia."

But that wasn't what the cat had in mind. She climbed over the book and put her front paws on Parker's chest.

Parker chuckled. "What are you doing, you silly girl?" She placed the book on a side table and began running her hands up and down Olivia's outstretched body. "What do you want, sweet girl—attention? Have I been ignoring you? Well, I'm sorry. I'll pet you. You're such a cutie patootie." She rubbed her face against Olivia's silky fur and murmured, "You're such a good girl."

Olivia responded to the petting for a few moments, then she leaped from the chair and began turning in circles on the floor. She looked up at Parker and mewed a couple of times in her high-pitched, squeaky voice.

"What?" Parker asked, leaning over and trying to engage the cat. Just then she heard a tap at the door. "Yes?" she responded, picking up Olivia. She watched as the door slowly opened to reveal Blaire holding a cat in her arms. Parker glanced at the cat, then took a second look and said, "Rags!" She hurried toward the officer and asked, "How? Where? Oh my gosh, how did he get here?"

"Did he follow you here?" the officer asked.

"He looks like the cat they brought in a while ago to search for explosives."

"Yes, but he was at the station when I left. At least I sure thought so," Parker said, petting him. She looked into his eyes. "Rags how in the heck…" She asked, "Where did you find him?"

"One of the officers out back said the cat wandered out there to the bird aviary, then he acted like he wanted to come inside here. Is he your cat?"

"No, my friend's. He must have somehow hitched a ride with us in the van. Boy, can he be sneaky." She reached for him. "Here, he can stay on lockdown with me." She took Rags in her arms and asked the officer, "Have you seen anyone or…?"

Officer Olivares shook her head. "Not yet. These stakeouts can be boring, but you know what? Sometimes that's a good thing." She gave Parker an off-handed salute and started to close the door, when Rags leaped from Parker's arms, hit the floor, and ran past the officer toward the back of the house growling.

Parker's impulse was to chase after him, so she followed him into what appeared to be Simon's bedroom.

"What's wrong with him?" the officer asked, trailing after the two of them. She chuckled. "If I didn't know better I'd think he was a dog alerting us to…" Suddenly she put her hand on her gun and hissed, "Get down! Get down!" She spoke quietly into her radio, "Window at south side of house—breaking in. Decoy with me, and cat."

Parker heard someone repeat, "Cat?"

Officer Olivares looked at Parker again and saw that she had Rags in her grip. The officer motioned for her to stay down, then positioned herself against the wall, gun drawn, waiting for the intruder to make his move. She acknowledged a male officer who stealthily stepped into the room, gun drawn, then focused again on the activity at the window. She was prepared to shout a command when Rags broke free and leaped from the floor into the drapes. They heard the intruder yell, and the drapes came down in a heap, exposing a man wearing a black beard and wielding a knife.

"Stop!" the male officer shouted from just inside the doorway. "Drop the weapon!"

The intruder glanced around the room and saw Parker crouched a short distance away. She no longer wore the hood, but her dark hair fell across one side of her face. "Yeah," the man snarled, "I'll drop it just as soon as I use it on her! Good bye, Rochelle!" he screamed, taking a few steps forward. Before he could follow through, however, Rags attacked again, knocking the man off balance. Calvin Stanley tripped and fell next to where Parker was crouched. She quickly stood up and backed away from him as the officers moved forward, guns drawn and aimed at the prone figure.

Parker picked up Rags and grimaced. "Oh no. Look at all that blood."

One of the officers started to turn the injured man over, then looked at Parker and said, "You might want to go into the other room, ma'am."

"Thank you," Parker said, walking out into the hallway with Rags in her arms.

She heard Officer Olivares say, "At his own hand."

Parker stopped and asked, "He fell on his knife?"

The officer nodded. She said, "We need someone to identify him. Have you ever seen him before this?"

Parker shook her head. "No, but if you want to take a picture of him with my phone, I'll send it to Rochelle. She and Savannah can ID him." She instructed, "Take that beard off him. That's a fake, as I understand it."

"Yep," an officer said, tossing it aside. He handed Parker her phone. Okay, send that to Sergeant Gray. He'll show it to Mrs. Whitcomb. I hope this isn't the wrong guy."

"I doubt it," Parker said. "Rags sure had something against this guy, and as I understand it, he's rarely wrong."

***

"Who's hungry?" Michael asked later that morning when Simon and Adam walked into the Whitcombs' kitchen where Michael was feeding the cats.

"You aren't cooking again today, are you, Mr. Michael?" Simon asked. "I'm kind of tired of cereal."

He grinned. "No, Simon. I'm not cooking."

Simon looked around. "Then who's making our lunch?" He looked at the clock. "Or is it breakfast time? I already had donuts. It's just ten thirty. Are we having breakfast or lunch?"

"And who's cooking it?" Adam asked.

"I don't know," Michael said. "We haven't met him or her yet."

The boys frowned at each other. "What?" Adam asked.

"I'm calling out for pizza."

"For breakfast?" Simon asked.

"Brunch," Michael said. "Are you boys showered? Are you packed, Adam? We have to go to the police station, then we'll leave from there. I know your Mom's eager to see you."

"How long have we been gone, anyway?" Adam asked. "It seems like a long time."

Michael nodded. "Yes, a lot has happened in just, what, forty-eight hours—two days?

"Two days?" Simon repeated. "Are you sure?"

"Sure about what?" Peter asked, coming in from the backyard.

"You fed my birds again?" Simon asked. "Sorry, Dad. I didn't mean to…"

"No problem, Son," Peter said, rubbing the boy's back. "You can do something for me this week."

"Like what?" Simon asked.

"Oh, shine my shoes, do my laundry, iron my shirts…"

"Daaad," Simon complained.

Peter put his arm around the boy. "Listen, it's been a rough week. You didn't need anything else to worry about, and I needed to keep busy. It's all good, okay?"

"Okay," Simon said. "Thanks, Dad."

"So what's for breakfast?" Rochelle asked, entering the kitchen. "Or is it lunch?"

"Brunch," Adam said, "whatever that is."

Simon grinned. "The good news is that Mr. Michael isn't cooking."

Peter punched the boy playfully, adding, "And that Simon isn't making sandwiches."

"Yeah, we're having pizza!" Adam said excitedly.

Michael looked around and asked, "Where's Savannah?"

"Here I am," she said cheerily, trotting into the kitchen. "We're having pizza?" she asked.

"Yes, sound good?" Michael asked.

"At ten thirty?" she questioned.

"You're complaining after what we've been served these last couple of days?" Rochelle asked. "Anything sounds good after…" she started.

Savannah shuddered. "Yeah, I still wonder what garbage dump that slop he tried to feed us came from."

Michael winced. He put one arm around Savannah. "All cleaned up? Feeling better?"

She nodded. "I was just talking to Parker."

"Oh, how is she?" Rochelle asked. "Bless her heart for standing in for me. I just couldn't…"

Savannah smiled. "Rochelle, you had been through enough. Parker was happy to do it. She was glad to help."

"And Rags," Adam said. "Rags helped catch that guy."

"Yes he did," Savannah said, petting the cat when he walked up to her.

Michael smiled. "Wade called this morning. He said to give you a hug. I told him I'm afraid you're already bruised from hugging."

Savannah chuckled. "Well, Parker asked me to give *you* a hug."

"Me?" he questioned. "Why?"

"Oh, I don't know, I guess just because she knows I love you and she loves me, so…"

Michael tilted his head, asking, "What?"

"I wonder when I can get my car," Rochelle said. "They told me they rescued it before the blast?"

"Yeah," Peter said, "they want to go through it just to make sure it's safe." He hugged her. "Be patient. Those officers have been busy taking care of the priority—you."

She smiled at him.

"Hey," Simon said, "they should let Rags do the sniffing. He's a better bomb sniffer than any old dog."

"Well, I sure would like to get my purse back—you know, my makeup, credit cards, and all," Rochelle said. "Your purse is in there, too, right, Savannah?"

Savannah nodded. "Actually, just my fanny pack with money, credit cards, lipstick, and my phone. How I miss my phone," she moaned.

Michael slumped dramatically. "You girls don't have any money? Do you mean I have to pay for lunch?"

"I guess you do," Savannah said. She put a hand on Michael's arm. "By the way, Parker said she saw us on TV this morning."

"What?" Michael said.

"You're on TV?" Simon asked, wide-eyed.

"Yeah, you know, those reporters and cameras and all that showed up at the old house of horrors? I'd almost forgotten about them. Everything became a blur."

"I know," Rochelle said. "I was so exhausted by then." She faced Savannah. "What did Parker say about it?"

"Well, she saw me with Rags in my arms. He was being a wiggly-worm as usual. I evidently said a few words, and then we were ushered off into the cars. The last clip showed Rags in the back window staring out at the cameramen. She said it was hilarious, actually."

"I want to see it," Adam said.

"She was able to rewind it and record it for us. She's going to text or email it to your dad's phone." She tilted her head and asked, "Was that your phone I heard, Michael?"

He looked at his phone. "Not mine."

"It's mine," Peter said. He handed it to Rochelle. "A text for you."

"Oh," she said, "it's the sergeant asking us to bring Rags when we come to the station later. He said everyone wants to meet Rags."

Savannah winced. "I don't have his comfy harness." She looked around, "Do I?"

"Dad bought him that new harness," Adam said.

"But he doesn't like it," Savannah explained. "The one he likes…" she chuckled, "or should I say that he tolerates best, is in Rochelle's car." She then said, "Oh, wait, my car's still here. I have an extra one in there."

"We couldn't find it," Adam said. "That's why we bought him a new one."

"It's in with my lingerie," she said.

"Oh," Michael said, "no wonder we didn't find it."

Savannah chuckled, then said to Rochelle, "Sure we can take him. He'll love that."

"Can Blossom go with us?" Simon asked.

Rochelle thought for a moment. "I don't know why not. She was a victim too, and a hero."

Chapter Eight

"I'm so sorry," Rochelle said, hugging Savannah as the Iveys prepared to leave a little over two hours later, "and I'm so thankful you were with me."

"I'm sorry too," Savannah said. "You did not deserve that, and I'm just glad you didn't have to go through it alone, only…"

"Only what?" Rochelle asked.

"Only, next time you want to have lunch together, let's go to a busy restaurant, maybe, or stay home or…" She looked into Rochelle's eyes and asked tenderly, "Are you going to be okay?"

Rochelle nodded. "Eventually. I think I'll have work to do in order to—you know—forget and forgive." She raised her voice into a squeak, "That was terrifying."

"And you handled yourself like a…well, with your usual grace," Savannah said.

Peter chuckled. "Pretending you were going to throw up on that pervert? Yeah, that's gracious, all right."

The others laughed.

"Well," Rochelle said, "I got my car back, our purses were intact, he's dead." She winced. "Unintentionally by his own hand." She took a couple of short breaths. "And yeah, I'm pretty sure I need to go into therapy."

"Really?" Savannah asked.

"Yeah, I think I might need professional help sorting through the doubts that have accumulated inside my psyche. I mean, did I even inadvertently do something to damage or contribute to the damage of another human being? That's not what I'm about. If I have that propensity at all, I need to know about it so I can…"

"Repent?" Michael suggested.

"Maybe," she said, "and put it in check. I don't ever want to be responsible for causing someone to go that far off the deep end."

"Oh, Rochelle," Peter said, squeezing her to him with one arm, "you do not have any propensity to ever hurt anyone, inadvertently or otherwise."

"Yeah, well, let's just make good and sure of it," she said. She hugged Savannah. "Goodbye, dear friend. I love you."

After everyone had expressed their heartfelt sentiments to each of the others, the Iveys prepared to leave. Adam and Savannah got into her mother's car and followed Michael, in his veterinary truck out of the Whitcombs' driveway.

“Thank you for riding with me,” Savannah said to Adam. “That was nice of you to offer to keep me company.”

“And safe,” Adam said.

“Well, I sure appreciate that.” She glanced into the backseat, where Rags slept in his car seat. “Rags sure isn’t going to be much company or much help.”

Adam looked back at him and chuckled. “No, he isn’t. He’s doing his—what does Dad call it—his seventh-inning stretch? What does that mean, anyway?”

Savannah shrugged. “You’ll have to ask your dad. I think it has something to do with baseball.” She smiled at the boy. “Did you have fun with Simon this week? You two get along pretty well, don’t you?”

“Yes. He’s my best friend. I think I’m his best friend too. Like you and Rochelle and you and Iris.”

“That’s really nice. I think you came along right when Simon needed a good friend. Your friendship has been important to him.”

Adam thought for a few minutes then said, “All good friendships are important, don’t you think so?”

“I sure do,” Savannah said. She chuckled. “I like talking philosophically with you.”

“What?” he asked.

"Well, I like the way you think things through. You're a thinking person. I appreciate that in a friend and especially a son."

"A son?" Adam repeated.

"Sure, you're my stepson. That makes you a step above a son, actually."

"It does?" he asked enthusiastically. "Like better than a real son?"

"Well, you are a real son to me. There isn't anything I wouldn't do for you," Savannah said.

Adam grinned. "Does that mean you would buy me a truck for my sixteenth birthday? That's only about three years from now, you know."

"Three years and quite a few months—almost four years." She glanced at him. "And no, I probably won't buy you a brand-new truck for your birthday. I love you more than that."

"You do?" he asked excitedly. "Does that mean you'll buy me a truck and a boat and a horse and…"

"Hold up there, buddy. No. What it means is I love you too much to just hand expensive things over to you like that. That's not how you help a young man build values and character. No, I want you to have to work for what you want—earn it. Starting out with an older used car or truck makes more sense, and, if you really, really want the expensive truck—if it's a priority for you—you'll find a way to get it."

Adam sat silent for several moments, then he said, "That was a good answer. It makes me feel…"

"Loved?" she said, smiling. "…like I feel, because you chose to ride with me today?"

After a few more minutes, Adam asked, "When are we going back to Simon's house for that bird thing? I heard Dad talking to Mr. Peter about it."

"Oh yes, Simon will be showing Clayton and Matilda at a 4-H exhibition in a few weeks. It's sort of a way for the kids to practice their presentation skills before the big fair in the summer. I think they'll have two exhibitions before the fair. That ought to give the kids good practice for the real thing."

"Will it just be for his 4-H group?"

"No. There will be members from all the 4-H groups in a pretty wide area. They'll actually have it at the fairgrounds where the annual fair is held. Simon sounded pretty excited about it, didn't he? He's going to demonstrate how to teach birds to speak. He has also taught them a few tricks he wants to show off. Plus they have experts there judging the birds for their condition and health. Your dad might volunteer to be a veterinarian on the grounds for the event."

"Cool," Adam said. "Simon said it's not only for birds, but there will be all kinds of farm animals—cows, sheep, pigs, chickens…"

Savannah nodded. "Yes. The avian project is new. It involves learning about wild birds as well as caring for exotic birds."

"But they don't have cat judging," Adam said. "Simon told me there are no cats allowed. I think that's just wrong. There are always cats on farms. Cats and farm animals go together, like Rags and Peaches."

Savannah chuckled. "Yeah, I don't think I've ever seen cats at a 4-H exhibit, or even birds, other than chickens. There are rabbits, though, and horses, but, like you said, no cats. They keep cat shows separate like dog shows. You've been to cat shows. Ever been to a dog show?"

"No," he said. "What are cat shows for, anyway? Yeah, I went to one with you, but I didn't really get it." He scrunched up his face. "I don't think the cats were having much fun. They looked kind of grumpy to me, especially those real fluffy ones." He laughed. "The only cat I remember having any fun that day was Rags."

Savannah chuckled. "Oh yes, he usually finds a way to have fun no matter where he is, doesn't he?" She thought about Adam's question. "I believe cat shows are strictly something the cat owners like to do. They want to show off their cats, have them judged against other cats. Those shows are designed mostly for purebred cats—you know, pedigrees. People raise purebred cats to make money and the higher rating the cats get at shows, the more money the owners can ask for their cats when they sell them." She glanced at Adam as she drove. "They have a household-cat category at most shows, so you could actually enter your cat, Tiger, or maybe Buffy or Glori in a show."

Adam thought for a moment and said, "I think being in a room with a lot of other cats and people would scare Buffy and Tiger and Glori, but Rags might be a good cat to show." He twisted a little toward Savannah in his seat and said, "Simon and I were talking about the 4-H thing, and he's going to ask his leader about us doing a program with Rags."

"You and Simon?" Savannah asked. "But you're not a member. You don't even live in the district."

"Yeah, but Simon liked my idea for having a cat as a 4-H animal, and he's going to find out if I can help him with Rags as a project. I'm going to send him a list of the things Rags can do, and he's going to read your books. Together, we'll make up a program of all the things Rags does. I'll try to teach him some tricks. You and Dad said we're going to Simon's 4-H program, so it would be no problem for us to bring Rags with us, right?"

"Do you know what you're saying?" Savannah asked.

"What?" he asked. "Rags isn't afraid in new and different places. He likes people—except those he doesn't like. Yeah, if the leader says it's okay, I want to take him to the fair. Can we?"

"Are you sure you wouldn't rather have a horse as a project?" Savannah asked.

Adam thought for a moment and said, "I don't know. I like riding, but I don't really want to take lessons and be all formal about it. Naw, I'd probably rather have Rags as my project."

She laughed. "Well, okay, but don't say I didn't warn you."

Made in the USA
Las Vegas, NV
29 June 2021

25689049R00128